The Wife's Ultimate Revenge

"From Deception to Deliverance"

Gail Morin

The Wife's Ultimate Revenge

Copyright 2024 © Gail Morin, The Wife's Ultimate Revenge

Disclaimer:

"The Wife's Ultimate Revenge" is a work of fiction. Any resemblance to actual events, persons, living or dead, or locales is purely coincidental. The story contains themes of betrayal, deception, and revenge, which are presented for entertainment purposes only. The actions and behaviors of the characters in the story do not reflect real-life situations or endorse any particular course of action. Readers are encouraged to interpret the events within the context of the narrative and to remember that it is a fictional story created for entertainment and artistic expression. Additionally, the story may contain sensitive or mature content that may not be suitable for all audiences. Reader discretion is advised.

Table of Contents

Dedication

"This story is dedicated to all those who have faced adversity with resilience and strength, especially to those who have endured situations of manipulation, deceit, and betrayal. May you find inspiration in the courage of the characters within these pages as they navigate the complexities of relationships and seek justice in the face of adversity. This dedication is a tribute to the power of resilience and the unwavering spirit that drives us to overcome life's challenges."

About the Author

 "**Gail Morin** is an author known for her compelling storytelling and intricate character development. With a background in psychology and a passion for exploring the human condition, Morin delves deep into the complexities of relationships, resilience, and redemption in her writing.

Drawing inspiration from real-life experiences and the diverse tapestry of human emotions, Morin weaves narratives that captivate readers and offer profound insights into the human psyche. Her keen observations of human behavior and her ability to craft multidimensional characters resonate with audiences of all backgrounds.

Morin's writing style is characterized by its authenticity, empathy, and attention to detail. She masterfully navigates themes of betrayal, revenge, and redemption, inviting readers on a journey of self-discovery and reflection.

Through her work, Morin aims to provoke thought, inspire empathy, and ignite conversations about the intricacies of human relationships. With each story she tells, she invites readers to explore the depths of the human soul and discover the resilience that lies within us all."

THE WIFE'S ULTIMATE REVENGE

Gail Morin

Chapter 1:
Introduction

In a quiet sunny neighborhood, Polly, Terry, and Patient's Daughter stand outside Mr. Darden, an old man suffering from Alzheimer's Disease. They will go into his house. The atmosphere is at once pressurized and goal-oriented as they ready themselves to be of service to him during a trying moment.

Polly the EMT veteran Bear the front line, Expression is the combination of determination and concern. Terry, her colleague, is standing there always ready to give a hand in need. Along with Tom, the second member of their team radiates calm and confidence, his presence alone being admired even in the presence of the unforeseen uncertainty of the incident. Patient's Daughter, the most apprehensive, she still holds up hope and is waiting for the latest condition of her dad to be announced.

The scene is set on a pleasant spring day, enjoying the bird chirping and leaf's rustling; as these are at polar odds with the dejecting work to be done. What is evident at Mr. Darden's house is standing in the ether of the ditch, emphasizing the gravity of the situation.

Every gang participant has something to contribute, their individual competences and experience are united by the common will to help the needy with care and compassion. Polly, being the physician that she is, is characterized by her great dedication and devotion to her patients. To Terry's colleagues, he becomes the pillar of certainty and unity that they can always count on. Grant, who has less reacting and more thinking, is a constant voice of calm when the crisis is upon everyone. Patient's Daughter represents a devoted family member who illustrates a family love and its durability throughout changes.

In their union, they are well equipped to face the tasks that make up the spirited adventure. In response to the warm smiles and covert nods, a unity arising out of their desire to help Mr. Darden lifts the air by binding them together through love and care.

In the unremarkable but well-kept household, Mr. Darden awaits their arrival, the skeleton and the vulnerability, which he experienced because of the disease, clearly showing the whole course of the disease. Behind the whole chaos and confusion that usually comes with his state, he is able to recognize and greet his caretakers with a glance in their eyes, proving the unbreakable power of human connection.

During their approach to Mr. Darden's house the team took a minute of quiet reflection, strengthening themselves for the trials that were waiting. Through deep empathy and concentrated attention on what is required, they walk forward, prepared to soothe the hearts of and stand by the ones who need help.

In the midst of the crisis, they hang together, their determination remains unshaken as they choose to take the road to healing and hope. Then Mr. Darden's pain-stricken journey begins, a journey through which caring people try their best to alleviate his pain.

The way Mr. Darden acts show in a clear and vivid way that he is dealing with distress, and this manifests itself in a disturbed mind and in an agitated state. Polly and Terry's first impression as they enter Mr. Darden's home be the messy and disorderly environment. It is as if the chaos within Mr. Darden is also affecting the environment around him.

The pendulous behavior and bad temper of the man cause Polly to worry something is wrong. One can almost feel his agitation as he scans, in vain, the world around him that is reduced to his messy room, where his inner turmoil is reflected in the disorder outside.

When Darden peeps out of the room from the back, he comes with his mood letting us his outburst of anger and frustration. His accusatory tone and rude mannerism to his daughter emphasize his buried sense of resentment and pain. He comes to the conclusion that she has cheated him and left him in ruins and poverty as well as destroying his self-esteem.

The more his unhappiness is revealed, the more apparent he becomes with Terry and Polly trying to reach him. Rather than showing appreciation for their efforts to help him, Mr. Darden flies into a rage, firmly convinced that instead of coming to visit him they are just tools of his daughter who wants to discharge him.

Polly's confidences to calm him down are faced with doubts and derangement. Mr. Darden's defiance and his active reaction to their coming only worsens the atmosphere and raises the stakes of the events.

By not recognizing his decline and his child's true attitude towards him, the remnants of his sadness and the defenses built around his heart become apparent. He watches notions of treachery and mistrust appear to him from every turn and it prevents him from trusting even those who try to console and help him.

His behavior is all over the place, and as the confrontation becomes worse, he keeps being more unstable and unpredictable. These emotions gain power and control like the beast that is hellbent on devouring every piece of him.

It is in the heart of the turmoil when the gravity of the events dawns on Polly. She recognizes that Mr. Darden's tirades are not only expressions of rage but calls for help, these mood swings being the only way he can catch somebody's attention and knock them into giving him a chance even if it's only when he literally has no place to go.

This is despite the many dangers and hostilities that is everywhere around them and yet, Polly does not lose her confidence to help Mr. Darden. She does not succumb to the intimidation of his aggression, puncturing through the veil of social conventions to see the fragility and the humanity back his ostensibly confrontational face.

In spite of all this, Mr. Darden's turbulent demeanor summarizes the complexity of the human mind and how a person can fall down as far as that. But it's a journey that Polly is determined to go through together with him, one step at a time, even though it is very hard for him to restore his health and cut ties with the past.

The hapless daughter, Emily, was at her wits' end, as she stepped into her father's house whose living room was a mess. Anxiety wrapped her heart as gazed to the things lie around. It was like a storm scene after the hurricane, with papers strewn across the floor, drawers left open, and the general sense of chaos spreading chaos in the previously organized place.

Her father, Mr. Darden, had been progressive getting more decline during the past few months. His mental blunders showed up in more and more regular intervals, and his previously sharp mind seemed to be now full of fog. Emily had provided help for him during the whole time, but it was obvious that professional care was necessary at that very moment.

Being there in the middle of the mess, Emily could not empty the sink of this feeling of helplessness. Trying to persuade her father to seek medical help was a challenge for her because he would argue that he was right and that he was ok on his own. Meanwhile, when he had failed to answer her phone calls and text messages, she already made up her mind and she couldn't procrastinate anymore.

Tears were welling up in her eyes as she looked at the EMT (the Emergency Medical Technician) who had reached her. She wanted to hear that everything was going to be just fine. She had to be convinced that her father would be fine, that at last getting the help he deserved would commence. Polly sensed the severity of Emily's apprehension, then gave her a simple smile and heave of the hands.

Together, they boldly penetrate deeper into the house, their steps resounding in the silence and the quiet. Every squeak of the board was as if it drew Emily's anxiety and increased her heartbeat that traveled in her veins.

Looking towards the storage room, Emily's heart beat quickened with anxiety and trepidation. She listened to the noise within, a rhythm of text and shuffle of feet. The sound of my dad's voice, dyed with depression and bewilderment, bounced off the walls.

Taking one deep breath, Emily stiffened her mind and was ready for whatever that lay ahead. She had to be sturdy for her father, to carry his shoulders to be the backbone of support he required in this instant of weakness.

With a swift move, Emily pushed the door open and her eyes immediately focused on her dad's figure, slumped there by the bedside amidst the mess. A deep furrow, encrusted with greasy worry and exhaustion, was carved on his forehead, and it seemed as though the whole world was threatening him.

"Father", she murmured with a profound mixture of worry and love. "Emily speaking! How are you? "

Mr. Darden's stance got stiffened as immediately he turned to see her and his eyes had a question mark on them. In a second there was feel of knowledge in his eyes, a flint of familiarity that melted my heart.

However, there was a sudden transforming darkness that appeared upon his face, which made his entire demeanor laden with suspicion. Bitter words of hatred came out of his mouth, cutting the air in a knife's manner.

"What do you want?", he growled, his word spilling out accusation. "Why are you here?"

Emily responded to her father's tone as if she saw the venom in his voice. She expected for rapport, and a moment of enlightenment in the middle of the thick mist that was all over his behavior and perception. However, she faced only prejudice and mistrust from other human beings.

"I'm here because I think about you, Papa," Emily said, her voice wavering with her overwhelming feelings of love. "I am concerned about you. I need to ensure that everything is okay."

Mr. Darden sneered and he looked at me as if he was annoyed. "You're here only because you want something from me", he sneered, his face full of the outmost disgust. "You are manipulative. Don't you always have an ulterior motive?"

Tears ran down Emily's cheeks. She wished that she could understand what her father was accusing her of. She had been making an effort to be there for him, and keep him going through whatever means she can. However, the pain of having to deal with his hostility and lack of trust that overwhelmed her, she now experienced an intangible sense of despair.

Polly somehow guessed the mounting tension that filled the atmosphere. Then, she walked forward to give a helping hand. She gently laid a comforting hand on Emily's shoulder and gave her a faint smile; her eyes mirroring the bond which now needed to be strengthened in this time of turbulence.

The two of them were standing in the dimly lit room, the oppressive quality of the accusations, leveled by Mr. Darden, undeniable. Emily had come to the realization that she couldn't compel her father to receive any assistance and that the final decision remained in his control.

However, when she got into his eyes full of resentment and uncertainty, she found the glimmer of the man he once was – a warrior with a good character, independent and with determination. And in that stance, she made that promise to herself to do everything within her power to find him his way back to himself, to the man she knew and loved.

Polly was her companion, and together they prepared for the difficult road they were taking. But she knew that the road would be filled with challenges to achieve the goal, and she had never regretted trying. But concealing the hidden chaos and sorrow, was the spark of hope – the promise of better day and sun, where only love and understanding would be the guide.

When the team suddenly entered Mr. Darden's home, there was an obvious sense of urgency and tension. A disorderly environment was the backdrop to their arrival, suggesting that Mr. Darden was in the grips of some kind of turmoil. Polly, Terry and Grant conveyed a look of nervousness, admitting the urgency of the situation to themselves.

The refuge, the home, the place of comfort as well as of routine, now looked to reflect the turmoil suffered internally by Mr. Darden. Papers were lying all over the place, drawers were hanging open, and the living room had the air of a mania in an attempt to find something that was lost.

Polly, the older and experienced head of the group, took the lead. Her voice was composed but powerful as she directed their next line of action. Terry and Grant quickly took positions behind, being ready to help with whatever they could.

"Polly knocks timidly at the door," the intro said this time, setting the scene for the work to start. Their coming was invasive yet motivating, the torchbearer of hope to recapture the space that was full of darkness.

"Mr. Darden?" Polly's voice, which sounded worried and tender in the stillness, reached my ear. Indeed, it was a small thing but appeared to be meaning their true willingness of giving assistance.

The house still remained strangely quiet, as if no one answered her subtle questioning. Despite the setback, the team went on with the great determination, moving cautiously into the living room that was joyous compared to the gloominess that surrounded the whole area.

Looking at the scene that surrounded them, it was one of utter destruction. Items were upside down, and possessions were disorganized, scattered in all directions. No one needed to tell that Mr. Darden's fight was not confined only to his deteriorating physical condition; it was indeed an armed confrontation with the opposing forces of dementia and depression.

"Polly" is the name she said, followed a soft and quiet voice. "Hey, we've heard that you're not feeling so good and we're here to help."

Gateless by the quiet, Polly and her team continued their way deep into the center of the house where the noisy sound of steps was echoing amid the maze of memories and feelings.

"We're getting down the corridor", Polly asserted her dictation as a beacon of guidance in the face of the uncertainty that seemed to envelop them.

When they came near a lounge office, the shuffle and movement sounds grew louder and louder, obviously Mr. Darden is there. The rustle of the papers was followed by the opening and shutting of the drawers, to everything each noise was a proof of turmoil which plagued him.

Polly addressed, "Mr. Darden?" her voice sounding as if she was in haste and as if she was overwhelmed by compassion.

The silence fell down as it answered with no-noises, instead, a heavy air hung in the air. It seemed as if all the four walls were holding their breath in expectation of Mr. Darden emerging in the open.

"Well, we would like to know if you're okay," responded Polly, her voice calm and decisive. "Your daughter's worried."

The door abruptly swung open and Mr. Daren appeared there in front of the messy splintered pieces of his once cozy bedroom. His faced denoted the opposite of what he used to seem, that of power and independence.

"My daughter's the reason I'm in this state." Mr. Darden declared with venom in his voice, as he sat there lax and engulfed by a tempest of feelings.

The team was very intent on continuity, keeping their main goal, that is Darden's welfare, intact throughout the discussion. Despite the complexities of Mr. Darden's situation, they demonstrated their intermingled feelings and professionalism, respecting his uneasiness.

"How's your stomach? Did you have food poisoning again?" Polly asked softly, looking genuinely worried.

However, Mr. Darden was overly suspicious and distrustful, a sign of the siege of paranoia that was usually related to dementia. His message was a pensive reminder of the difficulties other people with declining cognition could face in life and would have on their perception of reality.

"She ordered you to seize me," Mr. Darden accused in a quavering voice that was now tinted with despondency and dread.

Polly's efforts to calm down Mr. Darden and to explain the situation all in vain, his actions provoked by a state of disloyalty and suspicion. However, albeit the tumult and clatter, there was a flicker of realization expanding the distance between the patient and caregiver.

While the team put all their efforts to evaluate Mr. Darden's condition and help him get over through problem, they had to overcome many difficulties that challenged both their patience and confidence. Still, their dedication to providing their patient with hope did not break. A shining light amidst the confusion broke.

Finally, it was not just their knowledge and skills that taught them but certainly compassion and empathy—the cement which held their profession together. In all the moves that were made in the face of Mr. Darden's predicament, they realized the vitality of human connection during perilous moments.

Together, they were a proof of the ability and determination of teamwork, being inseparably bonded with the purpose of comforting and caring for the affected individuals. And as they got deeper into the house of Mr. Darden also came the feeling that the only way out was forward; they were ready and determined to deal with any challenges they might face.

Chapter 2:
Initial Encounter with Mr. Darden

When Polly and Terry made a way into Mr. Darden's house, there was an atmosphere of a subtle disquiet invest his abode. Before, the living room was the sanctuary of warmth and familiarity, but at the moment, it was a creepy, quiet clue testifying to the pain that engulfed its tenant. The piles of paper that couldn't be sorted, the drawers left open, and an invisible tension embodied the atmosphere.

Polly's soft knock at the open door joined with the empty silence that hovered all throughout the space. "Mr. Darden, is it?" she said in that clear voice tinting of care.

There was no answer, not even a whispering that moved the air above his head. Even though they were frightened, Polly and Terry each took a step forward into gloom, and they were only joined by their echoed footsteps.

"We heard that you are not feeling well and so we have come to help you," Polly kept on, her voice a calming presence amidst the pervasive chaos that surrounded them.

Her words seemed to hang about the room, unattended. The sterility filled the space and only broken by the whispers of the wind and the squeaking of the floorboards.

"Down the corridor we're going," Polly called out in a confident voice although she herself felt that there was something that could tell them that their earlier assumptions had been wrong.

Each step brought them nearer the focal point of the noise, their awareness now attuned to take in the narration of what will follow. The shuffle of footsteps, the clamor of objects being displaced, it all featured to a cacophony of chaos.

The sulfuric sounds were rising, and sped up as they moved towards the back room. The whole wave felt as if the tempest was right inside the cramped area, about to overwhelm everything nearby.

"Mr. Darden?" Calling out for the third time, Polly's voice revealed a note of concern.

The noises faded off and the silence seemed to conquer the room chunk by chunk, preventing oxygen from running freely. Polly and Terry glared sidewise at each other with their hair standing straight up as they put themselves immediately in the defensive mode with anticipation of the unexpected.

"We just want to make certain that you are fine. Your daughter is concerned," Polly soothed subtly, and her voice became a warm light in the midst of the storm.

Without warning and thus they were unprepared, Darden threw the door wide open with himself with his disarrayed and sad appearance.

"It is because of my daughter that I am here!" he spit out, revealing sadness as well as rage.

The blunt bluntness in his words made it tangible and reminded me (me) of the broken bonds that signified the world that I lived in. Polly and Terry shared a subtle look, signaling to each other an understanding of the endless suffering than Mr. Darden was harboring in his heart.

"She cleaned me out," Mr. Darden recalled, his voice quaking with rage and confusion. "Maybe, she just deposited it into her account instead of paying me the rent!"

Polly couldn't help but feel the pain every time she saw Mr. Darden's weary lines on his features. It was a pain that came of grief and treachery and he had to go with its loneliness company in the silent halls of his home.

"What about that tummy of yours? We heard that you've been going through the motions by throwing up," Polly inquired, having a soft but investigative tone.

Of all the responses, it was Mr. Darden's that had a touch of defiance to it which served as a reminder of the ramparts built in his heart. "Cold as she is," he spit out artfully, his words dripping with hatred.

Having made up her mind, Polly, approached nervously, her eyes remained steady despite the hostility that Mr. Darden exuded from his shaken self. "Is it ok if we check your pulse?" and she asked with gentle yet strong voice.

The heavy silence in the room spoke for the broken ties between Mr. Darden and his daughter who were such foe to each other. It had been frayed around the edges by years of anger and remorse, and a gulf so big it did not seem that it could be crossed.

Polly, reaching into her bag, made Mr. Darden to recoil away with her fear brilliance in the air between them. "What are you doing?" he asked, a malicious anger coloring his tone.

She uttered, "We use this to check your blood pressure," patiently, and her voice was so soft that it almost felt like it was caressing them despite the storms that threatened to break over them.

Mr. Darden's eyes suddenly became gentle and during the span of a second, they demonstrated that behind his walls of stubbornness and mistrust there were at least a glimpse of tenderness. She involved you in this, you know," he murmured, his voice coatings with disbelief.

Polly's loved is hope and she shares this sentiment with him, a proof of the pain that dwells behind his rough armor. "All she is worried about is knowing that you are okay," she reassured her, letting her words to be a sort of a gentle reminder of the love they still had.

Mr. Darden encounter gave me an eye-opening on how swiftly the human spirit can crumble, showing a store of resilience that had not been recognized before. With all the mind-boggling difficulties Polly and Terry were up against, they first-handedly experienced the healing capacity of empathy and understanding during trying times.

Mr. Darden, once a man with a strong sense of himself and his values, now finds himself sinking into a murky world of mistrust and manipulation. As he looks around his trenched, destroyed bedroom, there is an unusual mixture of anger, disbelief, and fear in his eyes. The room which I used to look at as a sanctuary suddenly feels like a battlefield where memories are divided by the present events in my life.

The words he used against his own daughter were as sharp as a knife. They were cutting deep into the air. He considers her as a financially ungrateful person, since from his point of view she promotes her own financial goals at his expense. The father and daughter's bond, which was built upon trust, is now torn asunder, becoming a tangled web of resentment and lack of trust.

Mr. Darden, in his opinion, considers the daughter as not the kind and compassionate caregiver she was in the past. Conversely, she is portrayed in such a way that she appears to be a scheming individual, one who is plotting his fall for her own secretive motives. His incomprehension of this betrayal eats at him, keeps his paranoia smoldering and drives him into a depressed and lonely state.

The blank spots in his past become swarming with the desperation of his deranged thoughts fighting deep-seated fears as he searches for evidence to support his theories. He battles the cruelty of the moment, sensing the incongruity between his imagined reality and the notion in his narration that his daughter is the villain.

Janice's destroyed bedroom symbolizes the broken mind of Mr. Darron. The floor is covered by papers, drawers swing half open and the bustle of disorder reflects the disposition of his mind. Every moved object, every wrongly placed item is a memento of the disorder that has crept into his being.

In his strong desire to revealed the truth his paranoia starts to take the biggest part of his life. Every noise, every motion is automatically a hint that it is a danger around him which further distanced him from his own house. The places he once found so comforting now take on a sinister and daunting character, undermining his confidence and calling into question all the things that had given meaning to his life.

His statements against his daughter are an overflow of bitterness and justice. It was not only the money, but also the dignity and the independence she had taken away from him, according to him. The notion that what he thought of as his own flesh and blood was capable of such deceiving level astonishes him deeply and shapes his future into vertigo of doubts and mistrust.

Though his child tries to pacify him, Mr. Darden is fixated on the idea that it should be someone else, and not his daughter, who is poisoning him. His perception of her actions is that they are hollow phrases just for the sake of placating him while she strives to destroy him.

The moment when the father and daughter confront each other, Mr. Darden's willpower begins to diminish slowly but steadily. His allegations are like a dark cloud hanging over their fractured relationship, giving a grim shade to their already broken bond. He lacks peace and dreams of the re-establishment of the relationship with trust and harmony, but the wounds of the frustration are too painful to master.

However, in this way Mr. Darden words demonstrate a profound lesson on family fragility. His daughter may shepherd him out of what she believes is the cycle of mistrust and suspicion, but he still doesn't recognize that these shadows of doubt that arouse the suspicion in him.

As he stands in his torn-apart bedroom, Mr. Darden is a man torn between love and betrayal, longing for the peace and security that once defined his life. Yet, in the face of overwhelming evidence, he is forced to confront the harsh reality of his situation and the painful truth that lies at its core.

The air around the house was heavy with uneasiness; one would have felt it even before turning through the front door. Although, from the outside it looked like any other suburban home situated among well maintained lawn rows and lattes alike houses. Nevertheless, with the glaring evidence of chaos and disorder, it can be seen underneath the surface that there has been a dramatic change in the affairs within the palace.

When the car stopped in front of Polly's house, the awful feeling has grown stronger. The front yard, that used to be vibrant and green, now had patchy and overgrown clumps, while at the same time it was reflecting the well-being of the family. The porch swing, the last of its kind, an eccentric remnant of the days not yet forgotten, gently twisted in the breeze, a tranquil scenery while a storm brewed just at the entrance.

Polly paused with her hand near the door handle for a moment, eyes looking around the room which had once been filled with valuables. The drapes in the living room were hung tightly securing very long shadows that playfully cast against the walls with a chilling feel. A background noise of voices was slowly forming in the air, like a murmur but thick and intense at the same time.

When she entered the place, the tension around her seemed to go up a notch, literally being embraced by her in a robotic manner. My living room, earlier bed of peace and ease, was now deeply wounded from recent meltdowns. The furniture was overturned and the cushions were scattered all over the room in a random pattern that had a story of the events that took place within here.

The sound of Polly's footfalls could be heard in the hallway, echoing in the dark and with the only other sound being the quiet shuffle of other feet and hushed voices. The entire house was seething with an unspoken anguish trimmed with a fear, like it was just keeping quiet and hoping for the next blow.

She walked deeper into the house and her senses were hit instant exceptions of chaos. The papers were strewn all over the place, leaving their corners ripped and creased as though they were overthrown in anger. The drawers hung open for no apparent reason, clothes and other items deposited on the floor in a jumbled mess that spoke to the chaos and confusion that had seemed to take over the home.

The air itself appeared heavy with caution, with hidden words and lingering feelings. Polly's heart raced as she was looking for an exit in the labyrinth of corridors, her pulse becoming quicker as she took every stride. Each alcove held the potential of finding something new, each corner a place of danger, while she tried to keep a calm mind knowing what was to come.

In the end, she found the center of the madness which is the door to Mr. Darden's room. The door was halfway open, the frog fastened on it creaked as if it was disagreeing. However, Polly paused for a moment, collecting her thoughts, before she grabbed the door handle with shaking hand.

When she went in, she experienced a complete shattering of everything she saw. It was as if my room had participated in the battle between the opposing feelings, leaving their cozy comfort far behind. Mr. Darden, with his face distorted by a combination of rage and -oh, just despair-his hands shaking with anger, stepped into the center of the room.

Polly felt pity for him, but the storm of emotions that threatened to encompass them wasn't sugarcoated. The air became suffused with quiet pressure as they positioned themselves against each other, two lost souls who found themselves afloat on a tempestuous ocean of turmoil, each hunting for a firm footing amidst the turmoil.

And it was at that particular point, where they teetered from the abyss of hopelessness, that Polly saw that the real fight was not externally in flesh but internally in the human spirit. It was just a battle between the forces that wanted to tear them apart and the forces that wanted to make their lives better and make them whole against all the adversities.

And there her hands were trembling, but in her heart was a resolution. Polly faced the odds and stood before the monsters as if she was reclaiming the light that had been stolen out of darkness. For it was in this cauldron of turmoil that she knew that true power was made, and that they would only return home as a whole if they would brave facing their fears.

Polly and Terry, both of them were in a tricky situation as they gained entry through the broken door of Mr. Darden's room. The feeling of tension was in the air as if it was full of energy and papers were all over the ground like dead leaves in autumn. Mr. Darden posed there before them, a vivid reflection of distress and agitation, his eyes constantly looking around the room as if he sought to find his way out of it.

"Mr. Darden?" Polly quiet, comforting in a moment of utter madness. "Our purpose is to support you. Your daughter is concerned for you"

Driven by bitterness, his comments were soaked with resentment. "She's the reason I am here in trouble!" His desperate voice broke down, making evident his anger and disappointment.

While Polly was trying to strike up a conversation with him, Terry was there to stand by her side, actually a silent pillar of support. Jointly, they endeavored to quell the tempest which was faltering Mr. Darden's shaken spirit.

"How're your stomach?" Sher's voice was calm and soothing, giving the impression of a rope thrown to a guy standing waist-deep in water.

Sarcasm and mistrust could be felt in Mr. Darden's statement as if it was ingrained on the air. "Like she would care," he said under his breath with the shadow of his thickening pride showing in his voice.

Polly did not give up. She stretched out an arm of kindness and she was willing to check his pulse. Yet, Mr. Darden gave defiance, his frightening look getting more and more hot like an animal that was pushed to the corner.

"What's wrong with you?" He had spoken harshly, with an accusing edge to his voice, as if the very admission of his feelings would be a weakness.

Responding to his daughter in a calm way, her voice was, however, full of understanding and empathy. "Here is the device to check your blood pressure," she said with a slight smile, the words a silent acknowledgement of their common humanity.

On the other side, though, Mr. Darden's paranoia dominated, and his mind seized to patterns of conspiracy and deception. "You set him up for this?" he left being absolutely furious.

Polly's patience was like a beacon in the darkness, it became the only reason for many hopeless people to stay alive and hold on to the hope of getting better. "She just worries about you," she consoled him, her voice an ointment to her husband's soul as the turmoil subsided before her eyes.

Mr. Darden's anguish, however, was an ocean wave shooting against the waters of rationality whose fears and distrusts aim to overrun every one of them. He pushed Polly to the wall in the flash of violent anger, like a raging fire which gutted every single thing it touched.

In the turmoil of what happened, Terry went to help Polly to the point of using long-standing knowledge of the field conditions. Mr. Darden however, was filled with rage, his desperation driving him to take a stand against those who were trying to save him.

At the same time the fight progressed Polly's eyesight failed, she felt as if everything was slipping into an abyss of darkness. Yet even during the most difficult times the shimmer of hope that threatened to fade away did not die.

And then, as much as I was paralyzed with fear and confusion, he appeared like an angel addressed to guard me from all the demons around. He had no choice but to conquer the vicious owner Mr. Darden, with his strong will being a hallmark of the human spirit which cannot dither in the face of fear.

In the aftermath of the face-off as Mr. Darden got beaten, Polly's sensation got to the fact that human heart was easily to be extended. Despite all the difficulties she had been through, she had seen the power of the human spirit, something more substantial than any hurricane.

The breath came into her body and as she collected her strength within her and a new injury grew in her soul. An in that instant of desperation she had discovered the true metrical of her own power, a power created in the forging did in the crucible of hardship and sharpened in the flames of the experience.

And hence, she, standing among the ashes of Mr. Darren's destroyed world, Polly mustered the resolve to push onward, to continue her travel on the winding road of goodness and grace. Truly, it was not the battles we fought that depended on us, but the decision of us who we are and our courage against the adversity, and in this, our compassion to people.

Chapter 3:
Confrontation with Mr. Darden

As Polly and Terry approach Mr. Darden's house, a shadow of suspense runs through the scene. In the room that was once brightly and evenly lit, there is now disorder, a reminder of the confusion in Mr. Darden's mind. The feebly and timid Polly's knock on the door echoes through the absence of words, a fragile attempt to bridge the divide between the doctor and the Alzheimer's victim who is lost in abstraction.

Polly's voice is gentle with a slight hesitation as if she does not want to ruin the only peace Darden has left.

In the room behind them, they hear the sound of papers being shuffled, drawers being slammed repeatedly, and the faint shuffling of feet. While they tread a careful path deeper into the house, the anxiety is palpable, infiltrating the mood and suffocating the air.

"Here we come, be ready," Polly announces this cheerfully despite knowing that uncertainty is eating up inside her.

In front of me the rattling of Mr. Darden's desperate search gets louder while turning a corner to the back-room Dreadfulness and melancholy is growing as the footsteps continue to shuffle and the papers rustle together, creating a rather uneasy nocturne of sorrow.

"Hey Mr. Darden?" comes Polly's voice from the depths of the mass chaos as a beam of serenity in the hurricane that occupies Mr. Darden's mind.

The next moment everything becomes quiet with the noise ending and the silence replaced. It seems very unnatural and surreal. Unexpectedly they are startled by the door opening which flings it all the way to the other side releasing Mr. Darden standing in front of him among the destruction of his ruined bedroom.

His eyes, tastefully enriched with life once upon a time, now convey a blend of anger and bewilderment. His eyes bore in them; blaming and distrusting, he churns out the accusations as he rants.

"My daughter is the reason I am in this mess!" Mr. Darden echoes with a pronounced bitterness, and each word is attached with a drop of malice.

The list of accusations becomes a river of hurtful statements, where his children are described as vicious serpents waylaying on their father. Polly and Terry glance at each other, their hearts being very heavy, realizing the sorrow of John.

"She took all my money," Mr. Darden muses in a quavering voice. "See! Told you she transferred the money to her personal bank account, leaving me with nothing!

Polly understands his feelings deeply – his pain expresses the discomfort of being abandoned and betrayed which is common to many. Despite everything they get hurled at her, she still remains undeterred, continuing to give him solace and support.

"How's your tummy? We heard that you're throwing up." Polly interferes, showing her voice as the balm that cures Mr. Darden's turmoil.

However, this is the character's greatest weakness because he is consumed by fear, and his anger is just a symptom of it. And with each move Mr Darden makes to help the girls get Claire out of jail, his mistrust gets deeper and he sees them as tools for his daughter's scheme.

"She bade you lead the way to take me away," Mr. Darden avows his voice laden with the despondency and apprehension of impending doom.

The pain of Polly's heart is pierced by the misery of his, her feeling of compassion being beyond any confusion and misunderstanding. She feels around in her bag, coming out with the blood pressure cuff as if to covey the notion of stability.

"With this we monitor your blood pressure," Polly says softly, bringing her voice into a sea of fear and panic.

Yet Mr. Darden's terror breaks, the more his grip on reality disintegrating and his moment slipping away. For Polly, in his eyes, she sees emotions not just anger and distrust, but also difficulties and vulnerability of the person who stands face to face with the ghost of his death.

Mr. Darden's imminent death prompts an explosion of fear, which soon lurches into an instinctive desire for self-preservation on his part. Without warning and entirely out from Polly, he pushes her body against the wall and his hands are anxiously shaking with a combination of fear and anguish.

Terry tries to stop him but Mr. Darden luckily isn't his ordinary self, and he uses his desperation to gain strength and sends Terry crashing to the ground with an awful thud. Polly swallows hard while she experiences the rush of fear and excitement though her veins.

Polly is just there at the flick of an instant as she sees that Grant is approaching, his presence a beacon of hope at a time when the darkness is enveloping the whole surroundings. And suddenly, he is there, a swift motion to disentangle Mr. Darden's grasp, his even motion a staunch contrast to the turbulence that envelops them.

And while Grant is hurrying Polly, that feeling of foreboding sinks into her, her heart captured by the fear all at once. What follows Polly's confrontation is also Polly's own personal journey to unravel both the physical and emotional wounds.

When she turns her eyes on the ruins of Mr. Darden's room, Polly ponders how many strings of human shortcomings and resilience are knotted into one against all odds. She is stunned to realize that she must not only fight with a specter of sickness, but also face the scale of human experience of suffering and the possibility of salvation.

In Mr. Darden's vision of Polly's outlook, there is lack of consideration and fear, and under the surface, there is plea for compassion and understanding. Then, while she is struggling with the stormy seas of his mind, she has to deal with what remains probably the most important question of all, the one that concerns what the notion of real healing is about.

As the dust settles and the echoes of the confrontation fade into the ether, Polly finds herself standing at the threshold of possibility. In the crucible of adversity, she discovers not just the resilience of the human spirit, but also the transformative power of empathy and compassion.

And as she takes a tentative step forward, Polly embraces the uncertainty of the journey ahead, her heart filled with the quiet courage of those who dare to confront the darkness and emerge into the light.

In the thick of the threat, Polly and Terry are in a delicate position of realizing and managing Mr. Darden's anger while also making sure their personal wellbeing is taken care of. And over the passing years, they have been trained on how to handle sophisticated matters and they use this training to dissolve the volatile environment in the home of Mr. Darden.

Polly, with her brown-eyed serenity and empathy, takes charge of the attempt to make a friend with Mr. Darden. However, her demeanor is full of hostility and suspicion, yet she keeps a comforting, reassuring tone, trying to convince him that they were there to help. Terry moves close to her and assumes a protective position as he watches over her shoulder with the intention of wading into the problem if the situation deteriorates.

As they walk more the house, the more confusion appears before them, symbolizing the chaos in Mr. Darden's mind. Paper thrown around the room, drawers unlocked in disorder —every detail reveals the turmoil that has overwhelmed Mr. Darden's life.

Polly's voice is louder in the stillness, a hand stretches out to Mr. Darden with compassion and comprehension. She is in touch with him grief and empathizes with his daughter trying to reestablish a connection between him and his daughter. While Mr. Darden at first displays resilience, this braveness starts to fall apart and his tender side begins to gleam underneath the tough shell.

Nevertheless, while Mrs. Polly is trying to bring the blood pressure cuff close to Mr. Darden, his aggression goes in a whole new level. Only his daughter's name releases the tripped waterfall of accusations and hatred aimed at the one person that he considers had let him down. The anger reaches to his veins and produces an aura of fear upon the room.

Terry steps in her direction to quietly emphasize that Polly and she are still together as they share the hard times. He steers Polly more than once and he is close ready to help in case Mr. Darden resorts to violence. Their allies bind them together in the effort of not being overwhelmed by the fine line of compassion and protection.

In spite of the fuss Mr. Darden has put to Polly, she has remained calm, displaying no sign of fear of the antics of Mr. Darden. A calm but steady manner, she tried to talk to him, underlining the need to discuss his health and wellness. Her words, greeted with doubt, still radiate hope – a point of no blindness in midst of around darkness.

Polly experiences the brink of her breaking point as Mr. Darden is becoming more and more adamant. Only the haunting presence of Mr. Darden surrounding her can equate to her dark cloud of pressure. Terry, who immediately understands the danger involved, is quick to act and his focus stubbornly remains thus despite the growing hostilities. A sudden instinctive reaction sees him trying to catch the criminal, his physical fitness helping him as he tries to save his partner.

In the midst of all chaos, her mind has rushes of different emotions getting tied together, which are anger, confusion and resolve. She is aware of the seriousness of the situation; however, she will not give up and she get this from her support team.

The next thing Polly feels is a wave of dizziness that envelops her, shaking her vision, and the whole room starts to spin. With Death snapping at her throat, she clings desperately to her wits, her hands shaking violently with the terror of it all. Her eyes fix on Grant as he appears in view, a saving sight that brings light into this murky darkness.

With assistance from the Grant, Mr. Darden is eventually put to a halt, the aggression recedes as the sedative takes effect. Polly is suddenly engulfed by a mixture of relief and tiredness just as the adrenaline rush begins to fade out. The entrail has cost her, both in physical and mental terms and still standing strong.

Polly and Terry relocate their ship, their resolution undimmed even as they move on from the hardships they have endured. Facing the challenges of the future, they still stay true to their objective of serving the destitute, a friend and a teammate closer than ever before. As they go ahead to transport Mr. Darden to safety, they know that the voyage ahead will be dangerous with many obstacles – but with Audacity and Spirit, they will take chances and address whatever the future unfolds.

As Mr. Darden's accusations get more serious and aggressive, the air in the room gets thick with his old-time stereotype and anger. Each word is filled with weight of the years of hurt and disillusion and sounds like a cry of a tormented soul, a cry of a broken relationship with his daughter.

As each hurling of accusations at Patient's Daughter builds the press, the tension in the room grows. Mr. Darden's quivering voice scathes with anger and rancor as he imagines a scenario of deceit and malevolence that led to his own demise at the hand of those he trusted more than his own kin. He uses phrases that drip of betrayal so that one can feel his pain even deeper. This, in a way, is the confirmation that his heart is still bleeding from the wounds made by his daughter.

The daughter of the patient cannot move. The expression of the daughter mixes anguish and disbelief in the face her father's accusations. The words touch the core of her beating heart, evoking joy and sadness differently. She tries relentlessly to comprehend the conflict between how much she loved him and the charges he made, looking for an explanation that will take away the weight of their accusations.

Polly and Terry look doubtful with each other as they observe how story is getting more and more twisting. The air becomes acutely tense as they deal with this delicately balanced situation, attempting to sympathize while at the same time, appearing to be impartial onlookers.

In spite of the chaos profoundly surrounding them, Polly was able to stay calm and composed, her training evident as she tried to cool down the situation that was escalating quickly. She appreciates the significance of empathy and understanding in taking care of Alzheimer's patients especially realizes that Mr. Darden's false accusation is not the result of malicious intent but rather a place of confusion and defenselessness.

In the climax of Mr. Darden's anger outburst, Polly finally finds her voice, though in a calm, yet strict manner, she attempts to shift their discussion towards his state of mind. She provides the comfort and empathy to fill the gap between the world and the illusion experienced by Alzheimer patients. This is where reality and illusion collide.

And thus, Mr. Darden is firmly rooted in his beliefs, and the details of his accusations get more obscure and disjointed as each minute goes by. He releases bitter words hitting her with treason and falsehood while his voice is shaking with the intensity of his feelings.

Patient's Daughter's mask starts to break with the intensity of father's accusations, tears peeping in her eyes as she tries to fathom the meaningfulness of dad's agony. She stretches out her hand, longing for a connection, but he turns away, the shattered remnants of broken trust do not allow for such union.

In the midst of the bedlam, Terry rises up, his voice unshaken as he endeavors to affect the situation; to de-escalate the stress levels of the room and bring it back to peace. He says supportive words and offers a solid foundation, his presence reducing the feeling of being lost.

However, Mr. Darden appreciates his words as correct his criticisms are a sobering aspect of the struggles of family life and the power of unresolved trauma. His words somehow linger in the air, as if a shade has covered the room and none of the three seems unaffected by what just happened.

When the dust clears, his patient's only daughter has to reckon with that reality and the depth of the damage it had caused to their relationship. The wounds would remain, resulting in scars that might bleach with time.

Those experiencing this scenario for the first time like Polly and Terry know how difficult the job of a police officer can be. The fact that the movie was made about this exemplifies the resilience of the humankind and the everlasting importance of compassion in the face of the adversities.

If they would pause for a moment, they would recall the need for empathy, understanding, and most importantly, regard for all patients, no matter their conditions.

Polly and Terry were both in a very difficult place as they worked out ways to help Mr. Darden who had been showing really abnormal behavior. One routine doctor visit quickly turned into an emotional encounter full of danger, tension.

Advancing further into Mr. Darden's residence, the mess became clearer, reflecting on emotions within the old man's mind. There was the sheets of papers splattered around the floor, and the drawers which were pulled out and more tense atmosphere in the air.

They were trying to keep calm, but Tess and Polly eventually succumbed to this unpleasant feeling. They addressed Mr. Darden in such a manner that their voices sounded genuine and sincere, although they obviously had a goal to reach him and melt the barriers around himself.

Their calls still rang through the still house, combined only by the rattle of items moving or the sounds of old furniture shifting. From the way in which Mr. Darden behaved it was obvious that he was in extreme agonies of mind and soul.

As they moved closer to the room, the source of the brouhaha became increasingly clear. The rustle of papers was heard increasingly and people occasionally made statements of indignation, punctuating them by throwing objects. Polly and Terry glanced at each other uncertainly, buttressing themselves in preparation for the upcoming ordeal.

With every step further to the back room, the tension was getting higher and higher, running a was like a knife edge on the air. They were well aware that they were about to set foot on unexplored territory, curiosity overshadowing the fear of the uncertainty that waited behind the door.

When they were able to get to the door, the view of the chaos that was on the other side, was something that was so not in the ordinary. Mr. Darden stood staring at the mess of his bedroom, not sure whether what he saw was reality, but feeling the mixture of rage and bewilderment. The clutter of the papers around him was aesthetic of his inner turmoil.

Polly and Terry strove to engage Mr. Darden faithfully and compassionately whose voice was soothing and convincing. They tried to show him that they were beside him throughout the process not just to reduce his concern, but to make him feel better.

However, the more she spoke the livider Mr. Darden became yet he refused to listen. He blamed his daughter for their rupture, admitting her defection and her perfidy, his voice oscillating with explosive passion. It was as if he had these feelings of resentment and distrust at the bottom of his heart, they were almost ready to devour him completely.

Despite different circumstances, Polly and Terry were not to be swayed from walking the road to Mr. Darden, so as to break the distance between his world and their own. They approached him with tact and touch of humanity, that no negativity would see the end of their efforts.

And their attempts to communicate with him were deterred by defenses as strong as the juggernaut he was. He flew at them with words sharpened by his resentment and deceit, these being his armor before his tender heart.

Beyond all the fear, the ones from them, and the ever-looming presence of violence, Polly and Terry refused to leave the Mr. Darden to his lonesome. They didn't waiver, resolving that they would remain standing there by his side, irrespective of the cost.

When the standoff started reaching its peak level, Polly and Terry teamed up against Mr. Darden, each side standing firm not to give in. This was a battle of the nerve and endurance, and a demonstration of the strength of the human psyche amidst struggle.

And in the midst of chaos and confusion, there was a faint glimpse of hope, as if a light shone in the dark. Despite the barriers that separated them, Polly and Terry refused to lose sight of their ultimate goal: in order to be ready to offer comfort and care to others, even if the situation is very hard for you.

And so, they pressed on, their resolve unshakeable, their determination unwavering. For Polly and Terry, the struggle to maintain control was not just a duty, but a calling, a testament to the power of compassion and empathy in a world plagued by uncertainty and fear.

Chapter 4:
Polly's Actions After the Confrontation

Polly experienced many different emotions once she came back to her state of calmness. She had to find a safe spot, a place to sit her mind and perhaps strategize what next. In a quick flash, she made up her mind to reach out to the place that she felt relatively safe- police station.

My drive to the crime scene was difficult and full of agony and despair. Polly's palms were sticky on the steering wheel as she maneuvered through the city with her mind spinning with the latest happenings that had changed her traditional life. Every instant its strength grew — the sensation of being caught, as if a shadow was hunting her and she felt it creep into the dark corners of her brain.

The moment she parked in the precinct's parking lot, Polly had a deep breath that she used to calm her nerves before she opened the car's doors. She knew that when she stepped into those doors, she would be dealing with a fresh set of difficulties as well as that she had to take that step in order to reach her goal — uncovering the truth and pursuing the right path.

With the bag of fast food in her hand, the precinct was her destination, and with each step her heart pounded in her chest. She understood this keenly and felt the importance of her act and how it was full of dangers by her direct involvement with the authorities. But on the other hand, she couldn't deny feeling the purpose which was the fire within her – a strong desire to take control of her life and seek revenge for the injustice.

Polly was nearing the reception desk only to feel a rush of anxiety. Officers hustled here and there inside the precinct; some voices echoing against the walls as they went on with their jobs. For a moment she hesitated, realizing she was probably making a wrong move by deciding to go over here, after all, she was already having enough problems with her troublous life.

However, she noticed Jonny the neighborhood policeman who was the man she had a difficult relationship with. In the midst of all the turmoil, Polly somehow managed to find a little bit of hope in her heart, as she stared into his eyes, across the room She suspected that he was the missing link, the very one who would be able to open the web of conspiracy that confined her existence in that moment.

Walking with an evidently single-minded intention, Polly headed for Jonny's desk, leaving in her wake the echoes of her footsteps that reverberated in the quittered halls of the precinct. The touch of the bag was an inseparable companion, a physical proof of the Tago offered to him. In that very instant, she prayed that their common past would be enough, so as to cross the gap that grew between them.

As she came close to Jonny's desk, Polly realized that there was unrest in the air and that the silence, which was hanging between them, resembled a curtain. He looked exhausted, losing more weight, showing more signs of stress and strain on his face. Nevertheless, she couldn't get rid of this sensation of care that grew inside of her, feeling she understood why they both were in that very same kind of situation.

Holding up a small bag filled with food as if it was a truce flag, Polly walked slightly towards Jonny and gave him a warm smile. There it was – the mingling of awe and hesitancy in his eyes, the disbelief that slowly dissolved into a cautious grin. In that instant, she felt a surge of pride realizing that such decision brought her here for help from him.

Once they were seated Polly was unable to help the feeling of exposure that came over her. Now she is publicly sharing her deepest feelings to a man whom she once entrusted with her heart, not knowing whether this man will turn out to be her lover or her foe. Nevertheless, on the contrary, there was an object of optimism in that conceivably, together, they might be able to find the solutions they craved.

As she herself was served food, Polly and Jonny started their conversation tentatively. The air was heavy with unsaid tensions and still unresolved emotions. On the other hand, despite the chaos, there was an air of camaraderie. A feeling that in a way those who were once united were still united, even if it was temporary.

In that instant, Polly was certain that in the midst of confusing disorder, she was not the one to suffer alone. In Jonny, she found a surprising companion, a counsellor who could tell the whole depths of her heartache and the gravity of her struggle. Yet as they sat together in the precinct, eating a meal, helpless with uncertainty, Polly learned that even if the future was unknown and might be dire, she would fearlessly contend with it, following the spark of hope that seared her heart.

Along with Polly, Jonny sat in their favorite Café where the mixture of fresh coffee and people voices seemed all the better. She stirred her hot latte and the warmth soothed her nerves as she moved into the space to strike up a conversation with Jonny. Today was the most crucial; she had to get information about police procedures and the case criminology without being suspectable.

Pleasantly, Polly began conversing glancing at her with a casual smile. Her words were filled with curiosity. Jane asked Jonny fake questions about his work, mimicking the interest in police activities. As always, Jonny excitedly recounted his case stories and what they currently do to get concrete results.

While Polly paid close attention, her mind was working actively, trying to draw useful information without giving away any suspicions. She gently insisted, with queries about the subtleties of evidence accumulation and the delicacies of the interrogation process. thorough of the discussion, Jonny told them about everything with evidence collection, and the problems of achieving a conviction.

Following the general discussion, Polly tried to steer it towards particular cases where she think maybe will unveil more about the way this enforcement system works. She pretended to be curious about the big high profile investigations but in the background there was the real causes of her interest behind her facade of genuine interest.

Keeping Polly unaware of his plan and being sure she not be suspicious, Jonny imparted his current understanding of police investigations. He emphasized the central role of high accuracy and the painstaking workflow of case assembling from the very bottom. Polly listened to his words greedily, logging away every single bit in her brain as new pearls of wisdom for later application.

Polly, though joking and jovial, sought to learn if there were any quirks in police officialdom by probing the situation. She was interested in the difficulties of collecting proof and the legal barriers they came up against during the matters they investigated. Johnny, a chatty person, offered quite complete views on the complex issues involved in the field of law enforcement.

The chat kept going and Polly seized all the opportunities she could to pick some of the valuable parts out of the conversation. She did this by framing her questions in such a way as to make sure that Jonny does not grow suspicious. Through her characters' psychology, she delved into criminal behavior and detection techniques that detectives use to extract information from suspects.

Having totally no idea about Polly's secret plan, Jonny was still enthusiastic as he recounted his experience with passion using the past tense and mentioned the most memorable cases and what it was like to work in the field of criminal justice. Polly's heart pounding, she leaned in closer waiting for each word from his mouth. As the words flowed in, her brain was filled with possibilities.

While the couple were intensely engaged in their conversation, Polly switched the subject to surveillance and the undercover operations. She asked Johny about the way of technology used in law enforcement and undercover operations as well as its challenges.

Jonny, who was always prepared to converse freely, contributed insightful and candid talks on the evolving landscape of policing, sharing anecdotes illustrating the use of surveillance systems and undercover operations. Polly took those bits of advice and filed it in her mind, thinking it would be neededin future as she moved on to look at ways of getting the needed information without alerting everyone.

As the conversation is winding to its end, Polly feels grateful that she managed to get all the essential information from Jonny, leaving him unaware of her true intentions. She thanked him for his honesty, but behind a smile of gratefulness was the truth of how proud she was.

Polly left the café with a great sense of achievement. Her mind and imagination were full of ideas about how she could change the world starting with her own community. Coming to this realization, she was more equipped than she had ever felt for the assignment that posed such a serious threat to her survival.

As Polly is caught in the middle of the tangled connection with Jonny, she walks softly on the crossing of professional willingness and personal reluctance. At first, she is attracted to John by his charms and politeness which make the border between professional responsibility and personal contract indistinct. However, he had an impressive appearance but couldn't detect any drop of dissimulation and deceit in his words and therefore, she maintained a blend of curiosity and caution in their interactions.

In their professional roles, Polly and Jonny are left with no option but to work cohesively with each other, coordinating on cases and exchanging information regarding their individual fields of expertise. Although Jonny has a background in law enforcement and Polly specializes in emergency medical services, these two professionals have a partnership that embraces mutual respect and joint objectives as its core elements. Collectively they immersed themselves in the work, laboriously unravelling every intricate detail of each case with accuracy and attentiveness.

Nevertheless, as her professional ties with Jonny grow more frequent, she gradually begins to sense more and more mysterious impulses from him. He doesn't display any of his vulnerability and arbitrarily hides his darkest fears. In return, this irks Polly who can't figure out his secrets. In spite of her professional skill of maintaining the objectivity required, Hanrahan cannot help but be intrigued by the secrets that revolve around him.

However, since Polly is not only a curious but also a very careful professional, she is equally aware of the risks associated with exploring too much of Jonny's private life. She knows that the preservation of professional boundaries is the key issue, especially given the close proximity of the work they are going through together. Through the life lessons she has learnt, she now understands the significance of having personal space that strengthens her sense of self, which lays the foundations of her relationship with Jonny.

She does not know whether she should be angry at him because of what he has done or admire him because of his devotion. On the other hand, her professional impact makes her do everything to seek the answers, to uncover the facets of mystery that cover the real reason why Jonny is acting this way. However, on a different hand, her innermost feelings of fearing what might happen if she accepted his invitation and explored his world of darkness are reasoning the message.

Along the way Polly discovers that she gets peace of mind in the fact that her job affords her a sense of belonging. As an emergency medical technician, she learn the art of judging and sorting the emergency line of care above everything else such as stability and bravery. However, it is Jonny that keeps her tethered to reality, giving her a sense of belonging even though she is unaware of whether she's in love or just feeling alone.

The Polly and Jonny team combines their skills and work together to use the knowledge to overcome the problems they face as they do so. Sharing the principles of justice and responsibility gives them a certain connection that makes it possible to find common ground despite dissimilarities in their backgrounds and outlooks. As individuals, their differences make them a formidable team that no evil powers can corrupt. They are on the same page as they seek loyalty and justice.

However, as Polly delves more into the depth of Jonny's personality, she chooses to look under the 'layers' and notices some 'signs' which indicate that there is more going on inside than what meets the eyes. His inscrutable attitude, coupled with the enigmatic tone of his responses, raises doubts about the authenticity of his personal brand that is constantly disseminated to the world.

For all her doubts, Polly finds herself captivated by the strange atmosphere that clings to Jonny, compelling her to explore his fascinating personality with an unchanging vigor. As each encounter reveals one more piece of his facade, she is welcome to it, adding to the disruption, which already threatens their relationship.

When Polly realizes the complexity of her feelings for Jonny and how everything is not clear to her, she starts struggling in her relationship with him. But with uncertainty, she remains determined in her fight to unleash the truth, relying on hers and enjoying through the labyrinth of their intertwined destinations.

Polly failed to shake a feeling that something was not quite right about Jonny, she knew from the evidence that she had in her hands that it was something that had nothing to do with her or what she bought. His behavior, which was formerly thought of as reassuring and heartening, now carries a sense of confusion, insecurity, and surprise. It was the evening at the precinct that started to blur when Polly saw that the way Jonny interacted with Lynn, his colleague, was not as she expected.

Whether it was the look in his eyes, the quiet conversations, or the way that Jonny's mood changed when Polly entered the room, it echoed warnings in her mind. She had always had strong faith in her brother and looked to his strength and steadfastness provide her with stability on the dramatic stage of emergencies response. However, today demons of doubt came into play and unlike before, it weakens the once solidity in the relationship.

Polly innate instincts gained from being on the beat for so long, whispered to her that something more was behind Jonny's late-night visits to the precinct than what was surface value. She was becoming more and more convinced that he was harboring some secrets, the very secrets that could tear apart their marriage entirely.

Polly was distracted from every little thing by Jonny's doings, as the days went by. She caught something unusual in his manner – those late-night phone calls, those rushing departures from the house, those inexplicable absences during weekends. Each new revelation was like adding oil to the fire of her apprehension, which increased increasingly till she decided to check further into Jonny's world.

Polly, decided to find the truth, and as a result, sneaked up for spying on Jonny's activities. She started her work by recording his movements with great attention to detail, as if she were a detective and had been dealing with him for quite a while. She was installed bugs and devices; she was acquiring his phone records and she was going through his mail looking for fault.

It was what she found that left her shaken right to her core. Right behind the mask of Johnny's erring friendliness and closeness to others was a vast network of lies and treachery. Her discoveries included covert meetings, encoded talks, and bank accounts which were not made sense of. His situation was similar to having two separate lives, one of which Polly was completely unaware of until the day he brought it up.

Moreover, the deeper she in to Jonny's dealings, the more she finds out the depth of his betrayal. He had lived a lie, spinning lies and half-truths that produced a tangled web, that engulfed them both. It was the most unpardonable crime that he could ever think of. This resulted in the total loss of trust, which left Polly speechless and completely stunned.

Notwithstanding all the disarray and distraction, Polly's resoluteness began to sprout in her heart like a steel. She supremely resisted becoming an onlooker in her own life or a servant to Jonny's crooked checks of duplicity. As she uncovered one truth after another, she steeled herself for the war which was to follow next, and was determined to fight Jonny to fully command her fate.

However, it won't be just a simple task to talk to him. This would mean the gathering of the courage, the need to stand firm and the spiritual level of willingness to see and acknowledge those hard truths. Polly understood that the road ahead of her would be full with difficulties and ambiguity, nevertheless, she refused to run away in the face of the risk.

With the awareness of the reason behind Jonny, Polly started making plans. She got in contact with her friends, sharing her private feelings with those she trusted and let them all know what was going on. They turned out to be supporters. As a team, they cooked up a clever plan to prove that John was the one who had tricked them and to put him in his place.

When Polly was digging out the dirty secrets of Jonny, she was dismayed to mine the disconcerting facts that blew her mind. The revelations of clandestine agreements, shady negotiations, and wicked plans that could spoil everything dear to her filled her mind. Yet the ray of hope was born in this darkness – the hope for mercy, salvation, and a new start.

Each forthcoming new fact only increased her power and her certainty to oppose Jonny and break free at all costs. She denied herself the role of a passive victim affected by circumstances or a piece for Jonny's selfish deceptive play. Rather, she tied her power in herself and use the help of her friends and her inner strength which might be stronger than the outer things.

As she stepped closer to the battlefield, Polly wondered about the dangers and unknowns that lied on her way ahead. And eventually she understood where she was – that friends were by her side, the allies were willing to go to the battle for her, for truth and justice.

And this way she gathered courage and conviction to hurl on confronting Jonny and unveiling his dark secrets to the world It would a fight for the ages, the battle between truth and deception, the freedom and captivity. However, Polly was prepared – she was ready to deal with all the difficulties she could come across down the road and finally emerge as a victor.

Chapter 5:
Jonny's Interrogation

Instead of shining light, the poorly lit interrogator's room gave the smothering fog of a tense atmosphere. John, with his strong personality, on the opposite side, from Polly, who had a combination of anger and anxiety or something. The room seemed to contract and expand around them, precipitating the gravity of their agendas and hiding secrets.

Jonny's eyes, like serrated steel, pierced at Polly with intensity that could even perform a torture. He leaned forward, his hands folded together in front of him, portraying a feeling of authority and purpose. Polly, despite the way it could be seen on her face, met him in his eyes with an undaunted will that did not give in even the victim of his questioning.

Their talk was on fire as their hidden intention operated electrical machine behind every word. To Jonny, each direct question seemed to be an intricately planned net for catching in a net of half-truths and deception Polly. However she answered his questions in a way which was incompatible with her externally expressed discomfort by noting her words very carefully.

The longer it went on, the hotter the room became and it felt as if the walls were closing in on them, like the trap doors on a hunting symposium. As the interrogative aspects of his tone become sharper and more searching, Jonny tries to untangle the scattered strands of Polly's muddled narrative. He was relentless, piercing her shield, constantly seeking any 'cracks' in her armor or any sign of weakness or vulnerability.

Nonetheless, Polly resumed her determination, which would not let her give in to Johnny's crushing doubt. Maybe with every step and second, she was becoming stronger and stronger, she was getting control over herself against his unstoppable attack. She was equally determined to match his curiosity for knowledge with care and precision while making sure that she revealed only what was necessary and kept the rest of the truth a secret.

The precision of their verbal sparring was sharp like a double-edged sword with each word being the calculated gambit in the game of a high-stakes cat and mouse. In his turn, the clever imposer Jonny wanted to open up Polly who was like a multi-layered structure and show her real self without masks. Yet Polly, who was only endowed by her willpower and cleverness, refused to be dissuaded, and stand generally firm against the psychological warfare in which Jonny engages her.

Through the course of the grueling interrogation, the air became choked with tension, the silence between them heavy with concealed insinuations and subliminal intimidation. The penetrating glare of Jonny was directed straight at Polly, scanning for the chink in her armor, or any sign of vulnerability, which he could tap to his credit. However, Polly never wavered, her composure unbroken, determination unchanged as she faced Jonny's inevitable blows in destruction.

At the end, Jonny was the first to give up; this appearance of being in a frozen environment was just not something he could handle anymore facing Polly's firm determination. There was a whole tempest of contradictory emotions going on under his polished disposition, the rigid shell of his reserve gradually giving way to the exposed fragile self that was inside him. And in that moment of vulnerability, Polly saw him for who he truly was: a man who goes as a captain of his own ship with terrifying nightmares and internal conflicts.

Questions they did not know how to ask and answers they could not hear had confused the intricacy of lies and secrets that linked them at the edges of time's gaping gulf. In the harsh light of truth, they recognized the ghosts of their past which they fought with and questioned whether they could be forgiven for the weight of what they had done and failed to do.

Sitting across from Polly and Jonny in the dimly lit café where the air was perfumed with freshly brewed coffee blends within a soft voice from nearby talkers. Those were the rare instances when you could run away from the noise of your everyday life and just relax with the person by your side.

Polly sipped at her coffee with a contemplative look when she took Jonny into her eyes. Her eyes had a kind of inner curiosity about them -- a curiosity that had been bubbling for quite some time now. Jonny's way of life has always intrigued Lana, just the way he deals with the variety of issues and complexity of law enforcement on a daily basis.

"Jonny", she started, her voice was full of gentleness but at the same time extremely piercing, " I've always wondered what war is for the front lines of law enforcement". Life will teach you "the only thing you must see, and the obstacles you must overcome."

His look has softened somewhat as he was catching on her words. He could feel her amazement, these need of exploration to try to understand his environment. I experienced dark and dangerous situations, but I also got a taste of some beautiful moments which brought light and hope to my heart.

"It's not a piece of cake," thought Jonny and his voice sounded somewhat tired. "It is not uncommon to encounter struggles and problems. But I find a lot of satisfaction knowing that I am doing something that does matter to me."

Polly gave a little nod while her eyes never left his face as she was paying full attention to him. She seemed to see the depth of his faith — the commitment that sustained and fueled him even when all seemed lost.

"I only imagine," she said with a reminiscing tone. "However, Jonny, what are the most alarming challenges that are relevant to your job specifically? The things that lead you to waking up in the middle of the night?"

Jonny paused, and though his forehead wrinkled slightly, he took the time to ponder what she had just asked him. It was after all a question he had often struggled with, a question that had in fact always been at the bottom of his professional path.

"I face the greatest challenge, at least in my opinion, of the constant struggle between justice and mercy," he said in a calm yet firm tone. "Understanding the complexities involved here means finding a fine line between justice and mercy, between getting even and giving a second chance."

Polly watched him carefully, as her unblinking gaze was fixed on him. She could always feel the weight of those words, the entirety of the stressful burden that he had to face every day. It was not a load even she could manage to understand, a load that paved the way for all his actions.

"And moreover, the human aspect of this, what about that?" she asked with definite curiosity. "The mental exhaustion that must arise after this experience, when so many horrible things are witness every day."

Every feature on Jonny's face had changed, and a certain flash of vulnerability crossed his expression. This was something he had failed at on many occasions and was the most difficult battle he had in his life.

"The human side of it... therein lies the hardest nut to crack," he was convinced, his clear voice now cracking with emotion. "It is about not being afraid of yourself, of not being afraid to prove yourself in the fight for justice."

Polly extended her arm and finally found his across the table. This was a very meaningful act of exchange as it showed the deep-rooted connection between them, a connection which had been established through shared experiences and a mutual understanding.

"You are not alone in this, Jonny," she said, her voice a comforting chord. "Here, shoulder to shoulder, we walk the maze of life's uncertainties trying to live and love one day at a time."

"You're not alone in this, Jonny," she said, her voice a gentle reassurance. "We're in this together, navigating the complexities of life and love one step at a time."

Jonny squeezed her hand, his gaze meeting hers with unwavering intensity. In that moment, amidst the hustle and bustle of the café, they found solace in each other's presence, strength in each other's embrace.

And as they sat there, lost in the depths of conversation, they knew that no matter what challenges lay ahead, they would face them together, united in their shared journey of love and redemption.

Polly was attracted to Jonathan, the cool detective, more than ever after she experienced the unsettling events of the last few days. He seemed to give her relief from her worries and also provided an element of intrigue. As the time progressed with each other, they were able to talk at a deeper level about how police functions and the details behind the criminal investigations.

And one night, at a coffee-shop with a very cozy ambience, I listened to Jonny, as he put his hands on the table and started talking with a low and ardent voice.

He then ventured into enlightening them on police disciplines and investigations, which they both found useful because they had never thought about it before.

He talked about the intricate process of obtaining evidence, where every minute detail as the least of all, bared the potential of uncovering the truth behind a crime. Every step in the investigation, from examining the forensic evidence to interviewing witnesses, was as important as the other one in making a cohesive case for the case.

Through Jonny's words, I could more or less imagine the struggles and triumphs that his line of work entailed. He retold the instances when it had been too difficult for him to sleep after seeing their indelible imprints on his mind. Polly reacted attentively with awe as he continued fervently and determinedly with each of his words.

The discussion between Polly and the police officer gave her a clear picture of the police department. The badge and the uniform became emblems of these humans who were guided by the spirit of public service and acted selflessly towards their community. The diligence on Jonny's job was visible as he commented on the tales and pearls of wisdom gained from a long career of the law enforcement service.

However, the truth was also that there was the darker side to law enforcement than what Jonny threw colored light on. He said frankly that overcoming the red tape of the department involved different paths in which sometimes justice was put aside for other things.

Notwithstanding the complicated nature of the work, Jonny nonetheless kept faithful in his belief that the law can create the necessary change. He talked about examples of both victory and defeat when the perpetrators were finally caught, but the pain never truly left victims.

Polly felt even more favorably for Jonny's endeavor as she understood it more. The endless devotion of the lawbreakers in safeguarding the law and seeking justice amid corruption was in itself awe-inspiring.

Yet, outside the professional, they also experienced a mutual appeal between Polly and Jonny. Sharing their thoughts and even at times some intimate feelings added a special spark to their relationship and created a connection that seemed to be something more than being part of each other's jobs.

To Johnny, Polly had a person, who knew everything about her life, of the complications standing before her as an EMT. Their friendship became for her a source of tranquility and sympathy in the world that was many times violent and unclear.

Upon leaving, and returning to her own room, she could not dispel the thought that this was the path she had never dreamt of. Thus, every time she conversed with Jonny, she was discovering more and more about life, all thanks to his generous and rich knowledge.

With no such indications, their nascent connection was destined to face an ordeal as they became part of a complicating network of secrets and deception that would make them question everything, they had been led to believe on regards to loyalty, trust, and justice

The development of Polly and Jonny's relationship as they navigate the complexity of emotions, goals, and power games shed more light on their situation. Weaving through the mysteries of the connection, it becomes apparent that veiled hints of hidden truths are present when deciphering deeper problems and hidden purposes.

Polly and Jonny's dialogue develops while the setting is in a caffe where the air is filled with a thrumming undercurrent of stress and anxieties. Under the guise of being casual, one can sense an undeniable animosity between the duo permeating the air like a silent explosion ready to explode at any given moment.

Their words have different types of meanings in addition to nuances and hidden reasons behind them. Polly, putting up an act of disinterestedness, seems to be hiding her real emotions, while Jonny is pretending to be callous, struggling with his emotions which are churning and boiling below the surface.

While their talk seems like sweet nothings and not more than greetings and casual conversations, the dance of words in these edges reveal unspoken facts and conflicts that still hang on their minds. Every letter has the soul of pain that did not come out and satisfaction that did not exist, which makes them real and profound.

Polly's eyes utter the susceptibility of her soul, revealing for a heartfelt moment what lies within her heart. She looks for an emotional come together and a feeling of understanding, and when it comes to her heart, she has thick walls to protect it from the hurt of previous deceptions and broken hearts.

And, Johnny carries with him his own secrets and fears, which are concealed behind a facade of confidence and grip. The are just one set of words that are full with ambiguity, his gestures are just veiled with the layers of deception, and he clanged for the illusion of power and authority.

Their converse seems to come up as naturally as a beautiful dance that has every move deliberately crafted to keep the truth in the gloom outside. But the created facades of feeling evince the seething emotions that come close to explosion through a deluge of raw intensity and uncontrollable passion.

The tension between the two is like the dense fog that it impossible to see through, that is thick in the air and blocks the way. They navigate around the topics that in the open would add tension between them , one always wary of revealing too much but not too little and risking everything that lies precious to them.

Nevertheless, for all their efforts to keep up appearances, these cracks begin to reveal themselves in the solidly laid wall of composure. Emotions overflow and they coming very close to destroy the carefully created equilibrium which they have established earlier.

Polly's voice is nervous and trembling as she touches the topic of tension and conflict and finally her speech is the mixture of fears and longings. She desires straightforwardness and genuineness, but she also highly undervalue the implications which come with sharing the true feelings.

Jonny's eyes waver, revealing a hint of vulnerability, as he holds her gaze, the façade that he has worked so hard to construct crumbling only briefly. Witnessing his self-control slip to and fro with the warring emotions inside his soul, he grapples with them.

Their exchange brews up like a labyrinth of hidden facts and unsaid yearnings for something more. Each word uttered, the unspoken yearsning and desires ring through loud and clear, moving them along the path toward the brink of the truth.

As the pressure builds and feelings climb to a new high temperature, they stand on the edge of a discovery which have what could change the whole world. A few seconds might be all that they need to realize that this is a moment when they have to either reveal the truth and put everything at stake or pull back into the protection of lies and deception.

However, the path that they choose will not only impact their relationship, but also significantly enhance their lives. The forge of their exposures sharpens the monsters that prey on them to the point where they can no longer avoid dealing with the wounds that remain raw and the want which remains unsated.

And as they stand on the threshold of truth, they realize that their journey is far from over. For in the depths of their shared vulnerability lies the promise of redemption and renewal, a chance to forge a new path forward guided by honesty, authenticity, and love.

Chapter 6:
Suspicion and Tension

Intrigue and anxiety took over when Jonny, Polly's husband, voiced his concern about safety, which aroused suspicion. The dialogue unaverred in this simple living room, where the evening light elongated the shadows across the walls, thickening the weight of their dialogue.

Jonny's brow crumpled as he uttered the words with utmost care, his voice showing deep concern for Polly's feelings. He had always been guardian like of her pride that came from the depth of his love and the underlying fear he had of losing her to the dangers that would swallow the world.

"Polly, I just can't get this out from my head," yawned Jonny slowly, his words cultivated but showered with fear. "Your work... it kept me concerned. The issues you confront, the situations where you get involved..."

Polly resting her weight on the old armchair's worn-out arm, gazed at Jonny with a combination of understanding and stubbornness. She was cognizant of the price of being an EMT which included operating during the wee hours of the night to respond to calls of chaos and distress, the moments of doubtfulness and fear. Yet, she had all the determination at her fingertips and the urge to be there for those who were in need, no matter what the cost to her.

"I understand that, Polly", Jonny replied, his voice firm, although stormy feelings wrecked within him. "But that's what I've got as a nurse. I can't just give up on people who need my help."

With his worry deepening, Jonny's mind began to wander in darker places as he imagined the possible threats, she might have to face doing this work. He was continuously tormented by the dull-throbbing anxiety of the future and the dark-ghostly shape of danger that seemed to hang over their lives like a shadow.

"Sometime I just think I'm doing too much, Polly." Jonny confessed, his voice fading a bit off at the end with a light shade of sadness. "You take the risks, you put yourself in the new situations... I'm not sure if I'm ready for all that."

Polly felt a squeezing in her chest, as deep as the bottom of the ocean, while Jonny's words were all-encompassing, like a crushing weight. She perceived his fears, his desire to protect her, but the same time she fought the inner realm of her sense of obligation and commitment.

"Jonny," Polly insisted, "I swear I'll be cautious!" she hugged him and then held his hand in a much-quieter show of affection. "I will not be reckless, and I will always prioritize putting my safety first. But in no way do I intend to abandon what my beliefs are about."

Their unfinished dialogue lingered like an unresolved chord, and there was a kind of tension in the air as they tried to make sense of confusing circumstances. In the dim glow of their living room, they were two seemingly lost souls left alone in the boundless sea of an unconcerned and unpredictable reality – love, however, kept them fixed together in spite of the hardships of life.

As twilight fell, Jonny and Polly got closer and closer though their hearts were hurting with unfamiliar fears that weren't dotted with known routes. The hush of the hours later caused them to cling on to each other, hoping for guidance and comfort in the midst of their shared doubts.

But beneath the surface, it is a premonition that keeps tugging on me. It looks like the challenges are yet to come and the trials are yet to be over. Jonny and Polly, who had declared themselves at and in the midst of uncertainty and tension, stood strong and determined just like sentinels, ready to face and overcome whatever the consequences may be.

When it comes to Polly and Jonny's relationship, they have to walk a tightrope between doubt and trust as their interaction is full of unrest and unease. Both are painfully conscious of the other's possible intentions, yet they should keep playing their roles that they have to act in usual in the course of their communication.

Now, Polly is in doubt what she believed in relation to Jonny after this incident happened. What's bugging her is the feeling that he may have had a dark side when she thought otherwise. All his pretty face, and expressions of her well-based on, there is a lurking suspicion at the back of her mind.

On the other side of the balancing act lies the loneliness of his life as a spy, which is lonelier due to its nature. He feels every single doubt so close, ready to blow up everything he's tried to hide for a long time. Certainly, he is compelled by her, is attracted by her heart and stoicism.

Their dialogues consist of secretive questioning that is tempered by the cautious answers, which allude to the following person's real goals or plans. Polly keeps a close eye on Jonny, hoping to either catch him in an act of treason or find evidence of his betrayal. Whilst, Jonny heavily describes his words, he takes into consideration topics that may reveal his agenda.

Even though caution is present in both of them, from time to time you will see authentic moments of intimacy between Polly and Jonny. They swap stories of adventures, and by this, they unveil pieces of frailty implying that everything is not perfect. In those moments the walls between them that the whole time seemed to be ready to fall apart return to life and are replaced by the trust that hangs in the air like a fragile thread.

Still, the closer they get the more their worries resemble shadows that loiter on the edges of the eyes. Polly just can't get rid of this unpleasant conviction that

Jonny is not sharing everything and that there must be something hidden behind his smooth surface. She finds herself scrutinizing his every word and gesture, searching for any sign of deception.

Jonny, just like John, has his own concerns that he needs to confront head-on. Today, he starts questioning himself whether Polly is aware of the truth or not, if she's seducing the cat to the mouse with him. He begins to doubt every step he takes and every utterance in her presence, sensing his uneasy whether her heart is with him.

Their relationship develops as the place where trust and skepticism meet with each step forward followed with a backwards retreat. They become each other, looking for holes in each other's armor, evaluating one another's vulnerabilities. However, a few inches below that on the surface, a prevailing tension wants to erupt, revealing the flashpoint of the bond they've formed.

More and more they find themselves going through the misty fields of their relationship and its high time they discovered the monsters coming out from the darkness. They get to the point when they need to know for sure whether they can trust each other, whether they are willing to let their masks go and reveal the painful stories buried deep in their souls. Only then can thecharacters be certain of their search for the answers they look for and discover the truth behind things that make them bond.

The greater Polly became suspicious of Jonny possibly committing some evil, the stronger was her desire to find out the truth. The notions of the preceding days had planted a seed in her brain, growing to an intricate web of suspicion and uncertainty. Still, she had to get the actual proof, which she was uncertain of, to make sure her assumptions were right otherwise she would not do anything.

Polly was affected, in particular, by the encounter with Mr. Darden, the Alzheimer's patient, who played the role of her biological father, and later when she found out about Jonny's connection with Richard Merrick. She just could not relax and believe that Jonny was telling the whole truth. She suspected he knew something but was keeping it to himself. His calm appearance and encouraging words, actually, now looked like a mask trying to mask a hidden truth behind the scenes.

Polly's days turned into a hunt — she was relying on gathering evidence, tying clues together and connecting the dots. She scrutinized cell phone records, account statements, and any other intel she could get hold of seeking clues that could suggest Jonny's involvement in malicious activities.

She followed the twists and turns of the rabbit hole, but discovered only a deceptive and deceitful process that exposed some shady transactions and questionable links. She carefully recorded all her findings, and as a result she came up with a sufficient dossier detailing the nature of Jonny's involvement in various shady deals.

However, the more she investigated, the more risks were revealed. Polly was aware that she was drifting into a precarious environment, playing on a high-stake game with the possibility of grave outcomes. She shared her secret with a few close people, among which was her trusted adviser, Grant, who shared the worries and promised her steadfast support.

Together, they carefully deliberated over their next steps, considering all potential risks and rewards from each act they performed. They were quite aware of the fact that they had to do their job with great sensitivity, in order not to provoke their nemesis and themselves to make themselves vulnerable.

Polly's relationship with Jonny became increasingly tough when she worked hard to preserve the façade of normality; at the same time she secretly struggled to unmask him. She began to view every interaction as a puzzle, analyzing every word to figure out hidden messages and deeper meanings.

On one hand, nevertheless, Polly was getting all the more suspicious of Jonny's mischievous nature as under his seduction his inherent darkness was slowly being exposed. He still made his day-to-day activities regularly, even though it looked like he did not notice the dark clouds building up.

But Polly did not do that either. She was fueled with a burning desire to find out the facts, even if it was at the cost of her own wellbeing. Her quest for justice turned into a one-woman crusade which was indeed fueled by a desire to keep the people she loved safe and expose those who mistreated and abused.

As the puzzle pieces began to fall into their right place, Polly's determination became unshakeable. She knew she was one step away from what she was looking for, one step away from making Jonny pay for his lies and revealing his misty activities. However, it was that with every step the risk grew higher and the stakes became great and unknown.

After a few days, Polly could not dismiss the whisper in her heart that everything was severely not right with Jonny. The once tamed and steady behavior of Polly was wildfire in a drought struck forest, it was so unpredictable and erratic, it enkindled Polly's fear and uncertainty.

It started with delicate changes of his charisma-so minor that average people might miss, but thing was like bright neon lights in the middle of the night to Polly. He was a bit tighter in his talk, his previous cheerful and outgoing demeanor now colored with an essence of caution. His laughter, which used to be a snappy one, suddenly turned into a fake one, lacking the indigenous mirth that always existed.

But what troubled Polly wasn't just his demeanor. It was the tales he seemed to keep for himself, trapped in the sadness. There were late night phone talks, whispers being stopped mid-saying whenever she came close and the undeniable fragrance of a conspiracy which grew in the room when she started asking questions.

Polly was trying to talk herself out of truth, to convince herself that she was overreacting and Jonny's behavior was a natural engagement of any kind of long-term relationship. But at the heart of it, she was always aware of that. She comprehended that something was undeniably wrong, that the pillar upon which their love was erected was in the process of being excavated by the rotting effect of uncovered secrets and deceptions.

Her doubts creeped through her mind like a rot spreading within, as they became more prominent in her head, finally aiming to devour her entire being. She started to doubt everything, and this included every word, every gesture, every blink of an eye they looked at each other.

And then came the lies—these millions and millions of little lies and half-truths and evasions that Jonny seemed to be able to so cleverly slip into the fabric of their relationship. He was a master manipulator, skilled at the art of deception, and Polly was beginning to realize that she may not have known him at all.

But it was maybe the developing feeling of isolation around her like some suffocating shroud that upset her the most. She found herself drifting without a compass, facing an uncertain and turbulent ocean with seemingly no safe haven in sight. It was hard for her to speak to anyone about her problems, to let go of the pressure of her fears, but she couldn't really do that - betraying his trust, for which it had been gradually eroding, was forbidden.

Finally, though she endured in silence and her doubts as the cancer that needs no excision only aggravated the very nature of their union. She wanted to touch and grasp the remains of that wonderful life of theirs, but they crumbled and fell from her hands like grains of sand, turning into nothing but emptiness.

As Johnny's odd acts got more and more frightening, Polly began to feel in her bones a malefic presence, as if there was a dark force waiting for her in the shadows. This was how she felt as she knew that she could not continue to live that way- in a web of lies and deception.

Yet, freedom is also terrifying— it needs courage to face up to the facts, that the demons exist and they shake under the covers of our mind. It would require her to puncture the Jonny-made cocoon of security, which surrounded them, to embark on the expedition of the unknown and find themselves a new way.

And so fully, and with a pounding heart and shaky hands, Polly decided to go after Jonny—to make him tell her the truth, to help her unravel the tangled web that began to dampen the air of their love. She well knew that the road was littered with danger and that an ugly truth about herself could bring down everything that she built. Yet at the same time, she was aware that living in the sphere of doubt and uncertainty was too great a burden for her, that she must pay the price of knowing, facing the consequences whatever they may be.

Chapter 7:
Jonny's Betrayal

Polly's heart broke and a chill penetrated her spine as she discovered the proof that tied Jonny, who she always considered her good friend to the hideous crime. She had found a labyrinth of lies, a spider web of corruption he built with tremendous skill which nimbly he wove apart from his charming appearance. With each piece of evidence, she uncovered she felt that it was a stab into her trust and an action that would be destroying her naivety and illusions.

On checking the files she had, she saw that what they did implicated Jonny in illegal activities with his fingerprints all over the accounts that reeked all all of dishonesty and avarice. The irony was, the man who showed himself as a loyal husband and dutiful police officer was not who he really was. However, now she saw through the mask and saw him for what he really was - a wolf in sheep's parade pretending to wear a sheep's garment.

As Polly followed the trail of the array of damaging files, she could not but dwell on the sense of incredulousness and fury that burned her inside. How has he done that? How can he cheat her so much, win her trust and values and then just throw them away? The depth of his betrayal sunk farther and deeper than she had expected, leaving her numb and drowning in a feeling of self-doubt that soon overwhelmed her completely.

However, in the midst of her various emotions, a force began inside of Polly and it was steely one. She didn't want to be a chess piece in Jonny's game neither as a bystander to his corruption. She knew it was time for her to confront him, make him realize that his actions had led to these consequences.

Having collected all her courage with nothing left to spare, Polly charged Jonny with the facts she had established, revealing the depth of his mendacity. The meeting was charged with such tangentiality that emotions were building as charges were thrown like javelins towards each other. In the very presence of her endless pursuit of truth, John's own mask began falling apart as his statements started contradicting one another.

However, as the time to confront Jonny approached, Polly kept on feeling more of the betrayal that was biting into her chest. The man she adored and confided in had turned out to be an evanescent, chimerical person, merely an artifact of her psychosis. She was unprotected and bare, fighting against the destroyed bits of her once-unbreakable trust.

Polly was out of her wits and in an ocean of uncertainty as she tried to get the situation under control due to Jonny's treacheries. The world she once called her home had been turned upside down, the very foundations of her existence trembled to the very depths. Yet in the midst of the chaos there was a little glimpse of something that seemed brighter than everything - the idea of redemption, of the new way that was unscathed by the falsehood and treachery.

Every single day Polly grew stronger, more confident that she'll be able to overcome the emotional and mental blow from the destructive fiasco of her betrayal by Jonny. And she would never allow anybody to define or limit her with their lies, not as the course of her future will be forever dictated by their deceitful acts. In place of giving in to the sense of defeat, she found resolve, a firm decision to overcome what had been taken away and come out a victor even stronger than before.

As Polly sailed the stormy sea of fake and real, she uncovered an inner strength in her she had never imagined. She made a choice to trust in herself, to accentuate her own journey of personal deference with bravery and compassion. Besides, she wasn't merely a victim of Jonny's infidelity but rather a survivor who had strength, power, and grit.

Polly's heart was marching like wildfire as she appeared in front of Jonny, her hands shaky with anxiety and intrepidity. She had his lies and his crooked ways in her hands, literally, a pile of papers proving what he had been doing behind her back. Jonny changed his surprise look to a stern hangout of defiance, as he grasped the magnitude of the issue at hand.

"Jonnie," stammered Polly's voice and the tone of her voice suggested that she was losing her strength but she remained determined. "We need to talk."

Jonny's eyes shrink and his jaw set as he knows there is a showdown awaiting him. He kept his icy composure, but scattered in his look, there was a flash of apprehensions, and a bit fragility that insinuated his outward confidence.

"What's this about, Pol?" Jonny's voice was even but there was a slight snap to it — it was clear he was nearing his limit.

Polly took a deep breath and braced herself for what was to be her destiny. She started to arrange the documents in an order, where each of them added new proof against Jonny's innocent involvement in the illicit business. All the conversations she had overheard, the deals she had uncovered, and the trail of corruption that led when she looked into Jonny became clear as day.

As she talked, Jonny's outer layer eroded away, his mask of indifference was disappearing, disclosing the person behind, a hedonistic, power-hungry and a stupid criminal. He sought to insert, to give reasons and explanations at this point, but Polly's piercing warning eyes gave him no chance.

"I trusted you, Jonny," Polly's voice had a trace of hurt, and the rage, which was contained in her eyes was evidenced by the fire in them. "I believed you. And this is the way you recompense me? By treacherously discarding all objective we value?"

Jonny shifted his gaze away, his shoulders hunched, as Polly's words burnt his soul. Certainly, he had been caught, revealed as the charlatan or fake that he actually was. Nevertheless, he held on to his last beams of honor and tightly clenched his teeth while he fought.

"I had to what I had to do," Johnny's voice was just a frail whisper but his words kept ringing in the vastness of the room. "I had done it us Polly. For our future."

There was so much irony in Polly's laugh. It was nothing of a smile, just bitter.

"For our future? Is this what you call the Johnny? The selling of the soul so as to get a position in power and might? How people give up all their values and ideals for the sake of this ladder?"

When Jonny spoke up, his silence screamed to the sky, his eyes fixed below, as shame filled him like a mighty wave. He had believed that he could cheat the destiny, it was him who always pulled the strings, not the other way round. At that moment, however, the realization of the magnitude of his immoderate aspiration came to him.

"I'm sorry Polly, Jonny apologized hoarsely, his speech interrupted with sobs.

"This was not supposed to end this way I always wanted everything to be good. For a moment, I thought I was capable of changing the system by playing inside it. But I was wrong. I see that now."

Polly's expression altered slightly to that of tenderness, which was then followed by a glimpse of sympathy as she gazed at the broken man in front of her. Through the whole, there was a touch of sympathy for that guy that use to be her partner, her friend, and her confidant.

"I forgive you, though, Jonny," Polly's voice was soothing like a melody, her words, heavy with forgiveness. "Ah, but sorry is not adequate this time. And it never will be. I have to suffer the consequences of my acts, regardless of how I detest it."

"Yep" was Jonny's reply, the look in his eyes mixing a sense of resignation and acceptance. He was aware that getting through this one would not be simple, a panacea he expected to bring back the glory he had destroyed. Yet, for the first time in an eternity, he experienced a faint glimmer of hope – the hope for redemption, for repentance, for a chance to make things back to normal.

In unison, Polly and Jonny embarked on a passage to reconciliation and retribution, seeing seeking to face the past errors head-on and to strive for a better tomorrow that would involve those they loved dearly. It was going to be a complete long road, a tough one full of challenges and difficulties, but they were passing it to the other side with courage and determination knowing that

justice could only be found in the light of truth and genuineness.

Polly's heart raced as she played back the recording of Jonny's conversation

with Richard Merrick. Every word was like a dagger, piercing through the

facade of the man she thought she knew. She listened intently, her breath

catching in her throat as Jonny's true nature unraveled before her.

As the recording played on, Jonny's voice took on a different tone, a tone she

had never heard before. It was laced with deceit, manipulation, and a coldness

that sent shivers down her spine. The way he spoke to Richard Merrick, the

ease with which he discussed illegal activities, it was all too much to bear.

Polly couldn't believe what she was hearing. The man she had loved, trusted,

and planned a future with was nothing but a facade, a mask hiding a dark and

sinister truth. Her mind raced with questions, doubts, and a gnawing sense of

betrayal.

She felt a mix of emotions coursing through her veins - anger, hurt, disbelief. How could Jonny deceive her like this? How could he lead a double life, one that she was completely unaware of until now?

But amidst the turmoil of her emotions, there was a sense of clarity, a clarity that pushed her to confront Jonny, to demand answers, to reclaim the truth that had been hidden from her for so long.

With trembling hands, Polly dialed Jonny's number, her heart pounding with each ring. When he answered, his voice sounded distant, unfamiliar, as if she were speaking to a stranger.

"Jonny," she began, her voice steady despite the storm raging inside her. "We need to talk."

There was a moment of silence on the other end of the line, a moment filled with tension and unspoken truths. Then, Jonny spoke, his voice tight and controlled.

"What is it, Polly? Is something wrong?" he asked, but she could hear the unease in his tone, the underlying tension that betrayed his calm facade.

Polly took a deep breath, steeling herself for what was to come. "I know, Jonny," she said, her voice steady, unwavering. "I know about Richard Merrick, about the deals, the lies, the betrayal."

There was a sharp intake of breath on the other end of the line, a moment of realization, of acknowledgment. Jonny's silence spoke volumes, confirming Polly's suspicions, validating her fears.

"I don't know what you're talking about, Polly," Jonny replied, his voice strained, defensive. But she could hear the uncertainty, the desperation in his words.

"Don't lie to me, Jonny," Polly said, her voice tinged with anger, with hurt. "I heard the recording; I know the truth. You can't hide from it anymore."

There was another moment of silence, a heavy, suffocating silence that hung between them like a veil of deceit. Then, Jonny spoke, his voice low, defeated.

"I didn't want you to find out like this, Polly," he admitted, his words laced with regret, with remorse. "I was trying to protect you, to shield you from the ugliness of my world."

But Polly wasn't buying it, not anymore. She had seen through his lies, his deception, and she wasn't about to let him manipulate her any longer.

"You weren't trying to protect me, Jonny," she said, her voice firm, resolute. "You were protecting yourself, your secrets, your lies. But the truth always has a way of coming to light, doesn't it?"

There was a bitter irony in her words, a bitter truth that cut through the facade of their relationship, exposing the cracks, the fractures that had always been there.

Jonny was silent, his words failing him, his excuses crumbling beneath the weight of Polly's accusations. He knew he had been caught, exposed for who he truly was, and there was no denying it any longer.

For Polly, the confrontation was a moment of liberation, of reclaiming her truth, her power. She had spent too long living in the shadow of Jonny's lies, too long allowing herself to be deceived, manipulated.

But now, as she stood face to face with the man who had betrayed her, she felt a sense of strength, of resilience coursing through her veins. She was no longer the victim of his deceit, no longer the pawn in his game.

She was Polly, strong, courageous, unyielding. And she was ready to face whatever came next, ready to reclaim her life, her truth, her freedom.

As the confrontation between Husband and Wife reached its crescendo, the air crackled with tension, thick with the weight of betrayal and deceit that had been festering beneath the surface for far too long. Each word spoken felt like a dagger, piercing through the fragile facade of their once idyllic marriage.

Husband's voice trembled with a mixture of anger and disbelief as he confronted Wife about her infidelity. His hands clenched into fists at his sides, the muscles in his jaw tensing with each accusation hurled at her. He struggled to comprehend how the woman he had loved and trusted could have betrayed him in such a profound way.

Wife, her expression a mask of defiance and guilt, stood her ground, refusing to back down in the face of Husband's accusations. Her eyes flashed with a mixture of anger and sorrow, a silent acknowledgment of the pain she had caused him, and the irreparable damage wrought upon their relationship.

The room seemed to shrink around them, closing in as the weight of their words hung heavy in the air. Every accusation, every bitter revelation, served as a painful reminder of the shattered trust that lay between them like shards of broken glass.

And then, as emotions boiled over and tempers flared, the confrontation escalated into a physical altercation, the culmination of months of pent-up frustration and resentment. In a moment of unchecked rage, Husband lunged forward, his hands grasping for something tangible to hold onto in the chaos of their unraveling marriage.

Wife recoiled, her instincts kicking into overdrive as she pushed back against the force of Husband's advances. Their bodies collided with a sickening thud, the sound echoing off the walls of the once-happy home they had built together.

For a brief, heart-stopping moment, time seemed to stand still as they grappled with each other, locked in a desperate struggle for control. Their movements were primal, fueled by raw emotion and the overwhelming sense of betrayal that hung between them like a dark cloud.

Furniture crashed to the ground, shattering the fragile silence that had enveloped the room. The air crackled with the sound of their ragged breaths, each gasp a painful reminder of the love they had lost and the wounds that may never fully heal.

In the midst of the chaos, they both realized the depth of the chasm that now separated them, a void too vast to bridge with mere words or gestures. Their marriage, once a beacon of hope and promise, now lay in ruins at their feet, the casualty of their own broken promises and shattered dreams.

As the physical altercation came to an abrupt and painful end, they stood facing each other, their bodies bruised and battered, their hearts heavy with regret and remorse. In that moment of profound clarity, they knew that their marriage had reached its inevitable conclusion, a bitter end to a love that had once burned bright with promise.

And so, they stood in silence, two wounded souls grappling with the wreckage of their shattered dreams, each grappling with the painful truth that some betrayals can never be forgiven, and some wounds can never fully heal.

Chapter 8:
Escalating Conflict

While Polly kept digging up the dirt for the sake of taking Jonny down, she treads cautiously into the more complex territories. It seemed that her intuition had put her on the verge of meeting the greatest challenge which was full of unpredictable difficulties and dangerous meetings.

Her courageousness to unmask the truth gave way to her walk on, disregarding the twitching feeling that was creeping between her subconscious. And, as her plan unfolded, the suspense became more powerful, and the cloudy shapes at the corner of her eyes got larger.

It was one of those fatal clashes when justice was being pursued by Polly that she met up with dark forces who were planning her ruin. She bumped into a blackmailer during this encounter who had a devious grin and a cold appearance. The air parted slowly with growing tension as their way became closer for a direct combat that would transform Polly's life forever.

The hitman, a hired assassin who is at an unsettling disregard for the value of human life, availed the whole meaning of danger personified. Through the power of his piercing glance, he broke down Polly's defenses, penetrating her inner sanctum, peeling away the falsehoods, and exposing her intimacy and weakness. She was now at the edge of the abyss, and oblivion was so close she could reach it out with her hand—at least it seemed so. Her willpower was the only thing that prevented her from falling prey to the dreaded danger.

Not only was Polly, a prey, aware of the imminent danger, but her whole bodily system was on high alert from the tense atmosphere. Every single nerve in her body sounded the alarm by asking her to be cautious and reminding her that passing on to the tragedy was not an alternative.

But Polly never ran away and never bowed up against challenges. With steel nerve and an ardent heart nailing her with rage, she straightened up her shoulders and met the hitman's eye firmly. Inside her there was a fire, a burning force to support the fight against the intriguing elements that aimed to darkness and to void the truth.

Flames of hatred erupted in the ensuing argument, with every motion and speech determined by a weight of things unsaid. Polly was in the negative edge of a double-edged sword, her every move planned but at the same time she was infused with a fantastic, animal energy whose logic and reason were completely uncalculated.

Amidst the strife and the muddle, Polly's heart and mind stood immovable. With a brave heart she denied to give up her voice and let the set aflame of justice be doused by those who wanted to be rid of it. She fought back with unbending perseverance, her spirit remained breath-takingly strong even when the shadows loomed inescapably ahead, and the odds were against her.

And yet victory has cost, a price that she has been left with for life on her soul. The wounds of war went deep; they were a part of her being, scratched there by the crucible of the battlefield and the flare of combat. And nevertheless, while undergoing the utmost challenges, she proved to be the strongest and the most resistant, just like a guiding light amidst the darkness around her.

And when the sun rose and thoughts were clouded, Polly grew up, firm in her mind, determined and unconquerable. Despite the difficulties and uncertainties in her path, she took them as challenges, and her confidence in the brightness of the truth was always mastering her way.

The fact that Polly was helped by new romance became a trigger for her to be more resourceful and selfish When she found out about her husband Jonathan's lies and illegal activities, she was dumbfounding for a while as the deepest recesses of her heart shattered into pieces and plunged her into a life full of danger that she never thought of.

In the process of the hitman's attack plotted by Jonny, Polly became aware that she could no longer ignore or look away from the challenges, the outcome of which lies in her own hands. As soon as her life was in danger, she made a partnership with a fellow traveler, who turned out to be truly reliable in the middle of the chaos. So, she found herself with a little hope to hang on to.

The collaboration between the two brothers was saved by their shared commitment rooted in the common goal of exposing the lies and corruption which Jonny had twisted the reality. Hand-in-hand, they began an arduous journey full of risks and despondency, fear gnawing the protagonists each step of the way.

Polly's unexpected savior turned out to be her rock, and his unwavering support became Polly's source of strength, as she went to overcome the darkness infecting her life. Under his tutelage, she discovered a way to draw upon her internal reserves of courage and translate her fear into a form of action, vowing never to be cowed by the shadows that appeared to lie in wait at every corner.

Their fight for justice was going on through a risky route that was full of traps and deceitfulness. With the more they dug into the background of Jonny's crooked world, they revealed the complex of lies and treachery that absorbed them both. However, the more secrets she knew, the more she became courageous and ambitious to espouse the truth about Jonny's reign of the terror.

Their quest for justice was somehow hindered by the dangers and obstacles that they came across in the labyrinth of treachery, cunning and danger, continually being on alert for signs of traitors and traps. Conversely to the odds raised against them Polly and her fellow new ally never lost hope of redemption.

They had to travel in mortal danger as the constant presence of the shadows of Jonny threatened to devour them. However, remaining steely faced and indented, they continued until it was their relentless desire that saw justice served.

With the new depth this time, they came upon different types of challenge from one them more dangerous than the other. However, in the process they encountered all those difficulties, Polly and her companion grew stronger their friendship forged in a furnace of experience.

They traversed a terrain full of danger, with the fear of Joe compelling every move they made. But the courage and determination, their minds were like iron that will never be broken nor effectively shaken by the pernicious adversity.

With every step they took towards the inner core of Jonny's criminal network, they knew that whatever came next would be their biggest obstacle. Nevertheless, despite the fact that they both firmly ran against each obstacle, their relationship only strengthened with more time spent together fighting the adversity.

In the court of the end, it was in fact their unwavering stubbornness and unbreakable teamwork that came out to be the greatest weapon to fight their way against Jonny's dictatorship. They fought with the wind underneath their wings and faced their fears in the process of becoming winners, their achievement an expression of courage and perseverance.

Disintegration of the threads woven into his mendaciously planned ploy renders him vulnerable to the exposure of the blackness within his felicifically calculated garb.

When the Jonny gang fails in the frame up of Polly for a murder, it is the epic turning point in his downward spiral thus marking the onset of his eventual downfall. However, in his effort to control the narrative by gaining an advantage, his deceit is uncovered by the truth as if the light is coming through the shadows to expose him.

Everything begins with the finding of key evidence that breaks down Jone's prudently built perception. As the investigators get into the case deeper and deeper, they come across discrepancies and inconsistencies which start to lead to the fact that Jonny's account of the events may not be credible.

Forensic evidence, witness testimonies and careful policing is the main explanation used to draw the picture of Jonny's guilt. The plot of the film unfolds and comes together, showing us how lies and manipulation is created by a person, because of his overwhelming greed and ambition.

As Johnny learns more and more and the walls start to close around him, it becomes impossible to breathe, as if he were trapped in a prison of his own device. This once great detective slowly fades away and turns into a powerless and weak individual who is ousted from his superior position and is left with no power and no influence.

Under the increasing glare of the investigation, the confidence of Jonny is beginning to disintegrate, with the result being his dispiritedness and paranoia. He is making a desperate effort to destroy the evidence but in reality becoming more accountable for his actions.

In the meanwhile, but Polly stands firm in her quest for justice, determined not to give up just when Johnny decides to use dirty tricks to make her look bad. In the face of corruption and deep distrust people start looking towards her resilience and willpower, it becomes their only hope.

With ever more proof against Jonny, the courts of justice get stuck on time as it were and the conclusion is Jonny's eventual arrest and trial. The hero once was unshakable is reduced now to a mere shadow of his former self and stand before the court to contend with the suffering his decisions brought.

In the court, the truth is brought to evidence for everyone to see, thereby exposing Jonny's crimes and the depths of his depravity. Speaker after speaker gives their testimonies against him, outlining a visual picture of a man who has a never-ending desire for power and wealth, his ultimate goal of which is to dominate all men.

In spite of his clever attempts to circumvent the legal action and to dodge the responsibility, Jonny's fall is, however, rapid and relentless. The judge gives a damning sentence, which sentences the man to face the greatest consequences the law can give for his crimes that hurt not just society but also humanity.

As Jonny being taken away in handcuffs the punishing voice of misconduct bounces through the halls of justice, ringing the warning bell of the possibilities of insatiable hunger and empty heart.

At last, it is not Polly's victory against Johnny that is the ultimate message of this frightening history but the truth is more powerful than the liar, and the justice will always be until the end of the world.

As the conflict between Polly and Joey came up to the boiling point, the pressure mounted and passions reached their heights. Polly, holding the evidence that stood up to scrutiny and her will as strong as iron, stood ready to face Jonny and tore asunder his fence of deceit.

A knottiness permeated the atmosphere, the air immersing itself with expectation, as Polly stood opposite to Jonny, her eyes glowing with passion. She had done a phenomenal job collecting proof of his betrayal. It was like untangling an intricate network of truths, he had made up. Every rebuttal and subsequent counter-argument only confirmed Polly's conviction, and she became even more determined to seek out the true culprit who had hoodwinked her.

But Polly, notwithstanding this, became firm and resolute, leading to a perplexion in Jonny's mind which eventually resulted to the boiling point of fear and desperation. He was aware that his meticulously built world was near the breaking point, and she had the ability to reveal to the public his deepest sins which were kept in the darkness for a long time.

With every word Polly uttered, Jonny's face started unmasking itself and revealing the helplessness and impotency that he never thought of existing. Finally, his efforts to evade and deny were faced with unshakable fortitude from Polly that resisted his neurotic tactics.

Things got worse as well. Every word was intended to push at the barrier that Jonny had constructed to conceal his real self. The voice of Polly, calm and dependable, cruised through the loudness, revealing the unadulterated truth to all. Her words seemed to come from the depth of what she believed, never having any doubts about it and not being forced to submit and deceive by Jonny's narration.

Everyone felt the tension build within the perpetration as the atmosphere thickened and the destiny of the truth was in the balance. Her tone was full of spiritual outrage as she revealed Jonny's betrayal, her voice making the accusation sound like undeniable truth.

The confrontation spelled the end to the order so painstakingly found by Johnny. When Polly's barbs were driven deeper into him, his defenses crumbled down and like some exposed to the full glare of the light, he was forced to face the reality of the situation. Polly's unbreakable defense undermined the defense of his reputation, and the big decision he was facing was making his situation even worse.

Chapter 9:
Final Confrontation

In the wake of the atrocious events that had happened, Polly was bound to the last line of battle, her heart aching with both fear and the single-minded purpose to win. Like a two-sided blade, the truth is in the air waiting to be used and tearing the idea of the normalcy which has been the only thing that has protected her for far too long.

With the erecting imposing doors of the police station situated right in front of her, she feels as if her burdens are weighing on her shoulders with the gravity intensification of its weight. She realizes that walking through those doors will disintegrate the glossy exterior which Jonny established as a tailored blanket around them.

Inside, the buzz of the station is palpable, and people glide hastily around in different directions, their faces displaying a bewilderment of expressions from total shock to disbelief. Polly's absence along with her, formerly, continuous presence here, since the day we first met her, has turned into a shade of unsureness. Her resolve is a lighting in the middle of the chaos, threating to absorb her in the process.

As she advances with every step, Polly mentally psyches as well as prepares herself for what the hurricane is going to bring forth and strengthens her nerves against the emotions churning inside her heart. She is fully aware that outing Jonny, hauling his crimes into the light for the whole world to see, will most likely lead to a host of undesirable outcomes, the effects spreading farther than an earthquake's aftershocks.

In contrast, entering the gloomy depths of the station is where she feels a purpose racing through her veins, fueling the expedition to that which was destined to happen in the near future. Her footsteps sound in the still air as the rhythm of her steps slowly becomes a drumbeat that keeps her resolve reinforced.

In the next station, Jonny, her husband, the man she once loved and trusted is waiting for her, looming in front of her like the demon recently escaped from her worst nightmares. The lines around the face, turns his eyes to flicker uncertainty, their depths.

And these seconds are the ones of eternity, suspended in the thin veil that separates the revelation from the oblivion. Polly's glare is enough to make him take her on, like two gladiators fighting in the arena, a sight that her inner fighting spirit inspires.

With her voice, the truth comes out sharp and smooth as a blade, freeing them both from the veil of deception they have been held in captive to. At a time when every word, every confession, Polly was trying to untangle the web of lies that Jonny wove around them, and draw a line between darkness and the velvet it created for their marriage.

Her accusations prove to hold true as he is stripped of his guise, unraveling to the revelation of his underlying evilness. But his argument comes off as weak in its face of the burden of proof, presented by Polly, which tragically testifies to his guilt.

As the circularity reveals itself, the room erupts into a cacophony of voices, the harmony of disbelief mixing it with the harsh stretto of accusations. Polly proudly stands firm like a rock in the midst of the storm, her voice like a light piercing through the darkness for justice against all odds.

Of all the took place in the middle of the chaos, the police chief came to be the symbol of the authority, his face being the mask of stoicism which gives no hint about the earthquake rising inside of him. He is fully concentrated on Polly's narration while Jonny tries to interrupt. His liquid eyes wouldn't leave for once.

As the minutes roll by, the walls resemble a prison as they symbolically and literally lose their space, the once significant flame being reduced to insignificant embers. The weight of his crimes winds him up, a huge load imposing on him that might collapse him by crushing him under its merciless weight.

All along, however, he was unaware that no salvation, no respite awaited him for the outcome of his deeds. At last came the climax, Jonny's nonsense of rules terminated and all his lies disintegrated in the brightness of the truth.

With her now shattered life in ruins, Polly finds comfort in the fact that justice has prevailed, that the implacable truth, regardless of how difficult to digest it is, has rescued her. Finally, and most importantly, what she is after is not the victory but the clemency, a possibility to regain the life that Jonny had snatched away from her.

And thus, it is as if the silence of the world around them has replaced the sound of the fighting, and from this battle with herself, Polly is born like a phoenix, rising through the ashes of her old self. To her, this glint of hope is a guide, a shining lighthouse in the darkness; it shows that in spite of everything, even in the deepest of the hardships, the human spirit remains indomitable.

For Polly, the final confrontation is not an end, but a new beginning, a chance to rewrite the script of her life, to forge a future unburdened by the shadows of the past. And as she steps out into the world beyond, she carries with her the lessons learned, the scars earned, and the unwavering belief that even in the darkest of times, there is always hope.

As society watches in near disgust, the once-admired detective finds himself in the middle of the media maelstrom and his reputation goes downhill quickly. The baring of his frauds and scams causes tremors throughout the whole precinct, cracking the confidence of both fellow officers and the public.

As a culmination, the authorities and Jonny find themselves in a confrontation seated in an ironic setting of escalating tension and general anxiety. As the corn of his misdemeanor is pulled out, Jonny's well-constructed image disintegrates and reveals the heights of his treachery.

The Jonny's illegal activities get more and more credit as proof surfacing on his wrong-doings, one piece after another. The invulnerable and unassailable police officer was now backed against a wall and soon to become an object of scrutiny, with every move he makes under the glaring spotlight.

When the threats intensify and close in on Jonny, he becomes increasingly desperate. He thus resorts to devious acts, attempting to shield himself and salvage his reputation. However, the effort appears to be a drop in the ocean while compared with the massive evidence that is emerging against him, and each disclosure just deepens the cracks in the image that he once had.

The final showdown of Johnny and his hunters is being played out in the dramatic standoff with the air charged with apprehension and the tension palpable. Jonny now explodes in a shameful rage as he finds himself surrounded by his former colleagues who turned on him accusing him of wrongdoings, unable to hide his widening realization that the end has finally come.

The horrific and disturbing interrogation room is converted into the last battlefield for Jonny, while the walls are closing in upon him as the truth slowly overtakes him. At this point, he has no place to escape to whatsoever, and there are no secure guarantees about his usually predictable future.

The unpleasant feeling of guilt that Jonny experiences when he encounters charges filed against him each one of them a powerful testimony of his moral decay. The man who used to be the respected detective is now nothing more than a ghost of his used to be self, the fact that he lost underlined by his fall.

The longer the interrogation proceeds, the more Jonny's mask is lifted, allowing the audience to see the fear and vulnerability under the hardened exterior like a layer of an onion. He becomes cold and his fearless attitude wanes with the continuous flow of information, which isn't able to stand up to the walls of truth.

As his last remaining hope of redeeming his self-respect, Jonny makes a final, desperate move to shift blame and responsibility off himself. Yet, his appeals do not reach a single attentive ear. His former allies have now become his foremost detractors, firm in their resolve to see him punished for his sins.

Towards the end of the process, Jonny begins to lose his defense and his guise is cut by the relentless interrogation. When the worldly truth hit him, John confronted the scale of his misdeeds, with his bright future gone without a trace.

The climax of the story serves as the final overturning of Jonny's dominance, which becomes the key moral lesson in the story with respect to the dangers of the unrestrained desire of power and morality compromise. With the consequences of his choice becoming more obvious with each passing second, he now starts to question whether the price he paid for cheating was worth the trash he brought to his name.

As a result of confrontation, we come to know that Jonny has fallen into the abyss, shadowing with tension those left behind in the precinct. When the dust has finished settling, the terrible extent of his fraud is clear and a path of destruction behind is noticeable.

However, out of the rubble emerges the silver lining as the authorities sprint towards redeeming the disappointing badge of honor, rebuilding trust and integrity. However, the real lesson here is that power is fragile and that human spirit is truly resilient in the final showdown.

As the tension had grown to its climax, Polly realized that she was right in the heart of a chaotic maelstrom that appeared to be self-perpetuating. The discovery of her husband's lie and the arrangement of the dark conspiracy against her came and overturned the last illusion of security and stability which had frustrated her. Though, in the midst of the confusion and inconsistency, just a little ray of hope gleamed in the darkness.

Side by side her new companion, Polly bravely waded through the covers she had been keeping for way too long. Polly's torment was in no doubt a permanent scar, both physical and emotional, yet she would not let terror rule her life. With her newly found courage and determination, she kicked off her amendment and regaining independence journey.

Polly experienced the shattering aftermath of the encounter, which she could not completely understand and which left behind a range of various, conflicting feelings. Aid of relief mixed with awe as she took in the magnitude of what had just happened. The fact that she had believed that her husband had personally orchestrated the most sinister plan against her broke her into pieces, exploding the everlasting love and stability she had felt innermost.

Amidst the craziness, Polly found a constant refuge in the undisputed help of those who were next to her. Another notable character was New Love Interest, who turned out to be a beacon of hopefulness and perseverance providing the arm that would steer her out of the dire situations she ended up in. The surpassed difficulties became a training ground for their relationship, creating bond that went beyond the tests they had experienced.

Hand in hand, they charted the course across the rough seas of uncertainty, coming up with the solution that freed them from the rot-forming web of deceit which surrounded them. As the days elapsed, they became more and more intimate. It was like they gained strength from their togetherness when they were fighting with their pasts.

The process of solving the issue was overwhelming and full of difficulties, but Polly tried very hard and not to give up. Armed with an unyielding willpower, she confronted her husband with the dark forces the once had combined forces to harm her. There was the moment where will collided with the person she was deciding not to cower in the face of adversity.

The disclosure of her spouse's involvement instigated the tremors of consternation, unparalleled even in those times of fragmented trust. Surface after surface that of respectability world began to collapse under the weight of the truth, and the darkness that was always underneath surfaced.

Polly stood at the crossroad among her own decisions, whose burden seemed very heavy in the aftermath of the confrontation. The path of redemption stretched out in front of her and was calling her forward to a future that despite its uncertainties was also infused with possibility. The Orphan Girl together with her New Love Interest as supporting force has begun to embark on a journey of self-discovery and renewal, aiming to restore her freedom and create a new opportunity for herself.

The end of the conflict was the final step in Polly's ordeal, but the marks left would be a lifelong reminder of the adaptability side of the human nature. At the moment of her greatest uncertainty, Polly seized the opportunity to confront the challenges that awaited her; having the courage and the courage of conviction, she knew she could overcome any obstacle.

The fact of Jonathan's true image, teaches us what can happen if we have a person that cannot be trusted and deceived. As Polly's suspicion continues to surface and she begins to unfold the series of lies spun by her husband, Jonny, the extent of his misconduct becomes frighteningly exposed. Initially the relationship that appears to be full of love and support is not what it is by means of hiding Jonny's face behind which there are the views about his despotism and corruptness.

Polly's initiation is rather naïve but as the incidents keep happening her belief in Jonny is being shaken by bit by bit. The Mr. Darden, a patient who has Alzheimer's disease, experience precipitates the change, completely disillusioning Polly about her husband's true self. The coldness and the calculated manipulation of the situation that he showed plus his strong wish to hold power over others gives Polly a shudder as she comes to understand the extent of his deceitfulness.

In the next scene, Polly brings Jonny in front of the police during the interrogation as he is accused of having betrayed her. Such a callous and uninteresting reaction of Mr. Bournemouth, as well as his threatening manner indicate that the interests of Polly are not a primary concern, which only strengthens the young woman's desire to uncover the truth, no matter what. As each revelation unearths the masks of their marriage, Polly abandons the house of cards with which she has been trying to hide her husband's betrayal.

Polly gradually gets into the thick of the investigation and she reveals that Jonny has thousands of relationships, going way beyond their marriage. The revelation of Johnny's secret dealings with Richard Merrick, a dubious underworld operative, leaves Polly's world in disarray, rendering her illusions of the man she once thought she knew into a blurry haze. Involving himself with the illegal activities along with readiness to sacrifice everything no matter what, paint a troublesome picture of a man whose mind was possessed by madness of wealth and corruption.

The Hannah's actions involving uncovering her real identity go beyond their marriage and remind us of the hidden danger of trusting others blindly. Polly's trip emphatically highlights the need to be alert and wary of those we think we can count on the most. Surrounding ourselves with daily deceptions is just another reason Polly's tribulations caution us about the value of always following one's inner voice and never becoming weak by losing our morals in the face of hardship.

On the strength of the unexpected friendship from Grant, Grant as one of the allies stand undeterred and sustain Polly with his loyalty and determination. Collectively, they begin the search for justice as they, more than anything, intend to lay the blame on Johnny's malevolent act and take their lives back. Through their bravery and the firmness of their dispositions, they give rise to hope as the world is often dominated by deceit and treachery.

The adventure where Jonny's character is finally revealed should be a warning bell for Polly, forcing her to rethink her values and acknowledge the corruptness of her marriage. Through this encounter, she experiences the inexplicable power of spirit and devastation, and emerges with a new sense of excitement about life from the ashes of her shattered dreams.

While Polly faces Johnny in the final showdown, she represents justice and forgiveness, there is no way she will be quiet or scared when he makes threats to her. The climax of the story arrives at the point when she pulls back the curtain and reveals the truth to everyone, exposing Jonny's maneuver fully and making sure that equality is promoted. In the end, Polly obtains triumph, restoring her sovereignty and creating the ideal path for the dawn of a brighter age devoid of lies as well as deceit.

Chapter 10:
Resolution and Revelation

Polly's win over the deception of Johnny brought the curtain down on the stormy phase of her life. At the very moment when she is in the aftermath of the events, and the truths unveiled, the burden of her actions falls on her shoulders as well as their consequences. Everybody seems to breathe a spirit of tension, a heavy atmosphere of closure permeating the chamber.

And when Jonny disclosed and the facts were in the air, Polly was faced a whirlpool of feelings. When the relief is combined with disorientation about the scale of Jonny's betrayal, it is a vice grip around her heart. She never thought that the one she had loved the most could be a cold-blooded traitor, a skillful manipulator.

However, in the midst of it all, there is also an inexpressible feeling of liberty. Polly had been so penetrated by Jonny's web of lies and ensnared in a marriage based on falsehoods and betrayals for too long. Eventually, she finds freedom. Finally, breaking away from his bondage, finally free to reconstruct her life and direct it into a fresh way.

As she recalls the series of events that brought to this point, Polly became aware how strength is of the human spirt. Despite the sadness and struggles she has faced; she has become more powerful and has ambitions to take the lead of her life into her own hands.

Nonetheless, despite the fact that she is enjoying life and enjoying her own liberation, there is a bittersweetness to her triumph. The legacy of an epic deception continues in the form of the painful scars which can never be completely healed. Yet, she is not under any constraint anymore, but the memories of their life together are the ones that accompany her like shadows in the depth of her mind.

Polly gets on her feet with the sadness of the past, and begins the process of her life formation from the remains of the old one. It will not be simple, it is what she knows, but she is going to make a new path for herself, one that is based on authenticity, solidity, and self-enlightenment.

Along the rocky way of her fresh-gained freedom, she leans on the assistance of her relatives. Her parents, the steady reference points of love and support stand by her side, whether she is taking the step towards the next phase of her life or not.

However, it is not only her family who mobilizes to support her at a time of crisis. Following the disaster, Polly was touched at the appearance of strange friends in strange places. Whether it's coworkers or mere acquaintances, a barrier of distance that used to exist has now disappeared, and they now offer personal sentiment of well-wishes, and fellowship, which acts a constant reminder that she is not alone.

Although weeks turns into months, Polly somehow manages to find her footing in this strange and unfamiliar reality. She rediscovers her long-lost passions, revives old friends, and fully devotes herself to the innocent version of her that holds no fears or doubts.

She, on the other hand, is a mix of both moments of acceptance with a brighter tomorrow and moments of uncertainty and doubt. The scars of the past are already healed, but the scars will forever remain to remind her of seeing through the trials of her life.

Polly's steadfastness remains immutable despite all this. She follows the path of the darkness in the back but decides to move forward to where the light lies. And during the process of that discovery, she finds something deep inside her, a power she never knew existed, the resilience of someone who has been through the most trying times in life and has survived those fires.

Polly, in the end, was not only a victim of circumstances but a warrior, triumphant over her fate, the embodiment of the undaunted power of human spirit. And though the road that lies ahead may be plenty of bumps, she will walk it in cheerfulness with the clear understanding that she is the maker of her own fate.

After the fall of Jonny, Polly is left dealing with the complicated issues of pardon and getting a conclusion. In spite of the extreme act that he did, she can't get rid of a vivid feeling of humanity that resists her emotional sense. It's him, it's the man who broke her trust, but she still muses about giving him a chance to redeem himself.

Sorting through the ruins of her relationship, Polly unveils layers of dishonesty and maneuvering that had those sometime brushed them under the carpet. For every disclosure, she feels a blade in her heart again, as the old wounds are being opened and the truth of their shoned past is being confronted.

Although, the pain of betrayal and heartache exist, there are also sparks of hope. Let it be the anvil of adversity where Polly senses her unimaginable source of power—an unconditional power emanating from adversity and growing from resilience. Indeed, it is precisely her inner strength which allows her to stand up to Johnny's treachery and insists on not being just a reflection of her shadowy past.

Nevertheless, in the midst of her confrontation with her fiancé's treachery, Polly is also keenly aware of the casualties left behind in the wake of it. Relationships became plunged in the extreme, friendships marred by the burden of unsaid things—one loss after another, these incidents raised the heavy curtain and showed everyone how devastating the cost could be.

However, in the midst of the disorder there is also an appreciation for the opportunity of renewal. Polly derives a sense of peace as her affectionate friends carry her through the recovery process with their undaunted support when dealing with the scorching reality of a broken existence. It is in these times of openness and unity that she will overcome the despair of the she is carried away by the beauty of a bright future.

The days blend into weeks which in turn merge into months. Witnessing this, Polly weaves a path of personal exploration and restoration. She takes a dive into the chambers of her mind, staring in the eyes the nightmares that once held her captive and remains triumphant, more resilient as a result.

Yet the process of recovery, which Polly embarks on, is besides not simple at all. There will be the failures and problems, instances when you will want to give up; there will be a time to be in despair and doubt of yourself. However, under the intense pressure of difficulties she summons up the inner resources to go on with her life, to transcend the ashes of her previous existence and to take with her the inspiration of the future.

For Polly, the journey toward healing is not just about moving on—it is about reclaiming her sense of self, about forging a path forward on her own terms. And as she stands on the precipice of a new chapter in her life, she knows that the greatest triumph lies not in the victory over her adversaries, but in the resilience of the human spirit—a resilience that has carried her through the darkest of nights and into the dawn of a new day.

The disclosure that Jonny's malfeasance could have been prevented shook the police department and the surrounding community as if an earthquake killed the faith and resilience that had previously been regarded as immovable. As the news of his participation in dishonest deeds were heard time and again, brought by the wind like fire, silence and caution have surrounded us in the precinct, darkening every action and decision we have made, including the arrests under his command.

The climate in the police department was electric with the sense of fear and anxiety. Previously, they had shared a bond, but now they turned around, looking at each other with mistrust, attempting to discern others' motives from every action and guess, who else (might be harboring) something behind (a mask of) authority.

To the majority of officers who had formerly seen Jonny as a mentor and commander, the disclosure was a flagrant violation of the worst kind.

It was very difficult for the fans to put together the picture of the devoted detective that they worshipped and the reality of a man behind the scenes who was into sleaze and twisted plots.

On hearing the news from the precinct, the whole community was stunned by not only the gravity of the news but also the fact that it actually happened. For years they had depended upon the protective duty and safety offered by the members of the uniform, trusting in their veracity and virtue. To my detriment, I am now bereft of that confidence, and left with feelings of betrayal and disbelief.

Jonny's actions brought on ripples which rolled far beyond, stigmatizing the law enforcement and anybody who had a little faith in the very conception of justice. People started to wonder how many other officers were involved in the intricate web of lies and uncleanly situations.

The middle of it all, the media took the scandal in the running loud of the scandal, earning more attention for the public and making the news more sensational. The headlines called for accusations while the pundits pontificated endlessly about the crisis in the image of the police, with the citizens demanding answers as well as accountability and justice.

The police department subjected itself to investigations, and committees were formed, and reforms were proposed, all aimed at regaining public trust and integrity lost. Officers were exposed to, and in turn exposed to, and their actions weighed under the harsh scrutiny of public eye.

For Johnny, the repercussion was the fastest and the most awful. Denied his badge and the authority which used to mean everything to him, he was pushed out of the organization for which he used to have great passion. He was left with his fame in tatters, his career ruined, and his life completely uncertain.

However, despite the destruction on one man terror actions, there were those who did not allow one person to define them. Despite the tortuous circumstances, the officers refused to abandon their creed, steadily trying to restore the dignity that had been drawn into question. Citizens were strong enough to stick together, deciding to defend their representatives from wrongdoing by demanding for more transparency and accountability.

The knowledge of Jonny's criminal behaviour, which in the end became a reminder of how easily we can be fooled and that integrity is the cornerstone of law enforcement. It was a lesson well learned for all the officials involved who, however, had to deal with the reality of corruption and the difficulty of rebuilding what had been destroyed. These challenges emerged, however, was also an opportunity for them to strengthen their resolve and remain steadfast in their commitment to justice, accountability, and a search for truth.

As a result of Jonny's downfall and deeply destructive effects, the police department was left with many different issues to navigate, ranging from the accountability and transparency of the police to the reformation of the institution. Through the internal probes, the departmental mechanisms were literally taken apart to reveal the deep rooted problems that were ignored for long and never properly addressed.

As the bright spotlight of media attention made the life of officers even more stressful, they faced increased pressure to demonstrate their devotion to the laws and their communal service. For most of them, it was a test of character and resolute, an opportunity to confirm their devotedness to the values that have always motivated them to a career of law enforcement.

Within the community impact of Jonny's failure reached far beyond the single occurrence and triggered discussions about power, privilege, and need for more transparency and accountability in law enforcement. Protesters and community leaders used the moment to insist on radical changes in the field of policing, in which activists asked for measures to equalize racial disparities, to improve police and community relations, and regulate the oversight mechanisms.

On the one hand, some people used that moment to achieve their own gains by misusing public anger to push against people of opposing ideas or to take revenge. Hearsay and speculations that are loaded with doubts regarding the motives of the people involved compromised the level of trust and created more animosity among the community.

Within the halls of power, officials and policymakers were in a rush to react to the crisis, trying to exhibit their concern, willingness to change and people trust back. The task forces were established, hearings were organized, and proposals for the revolutionary changes in policing operations were brought forward to be discussed and analyzed.

However, among these tempests of uncertainties and chaos, the rays of hope and resilience shone through. Grassroots groups took off upon hearing that someone somewhere had been shot and killed by a policeman. These groups began to organize community forums, host dialogues between the police and the residents and advocate for policies that would not only tackle the issue of accountability but also transparency.

Among the ranks of the police department, a new batch of young leaders has appeared who inherently advocate to pursue the path of justice and equality. They understood that it would take more than just words and words spoken and promises – it would require actions, meaningful engagement and courage to face hard and painful truths.

As the dust began to settle and the initial shock of Jonny's downfall faded, the real work of rebuilding and reforming began in earnest. It was a journey fraught with challenges and obstacles, but it was also a journey filled with opportunity – an opportunity to forge a new path forward, one rooted in justice, equity, and the shared values of community and accountability.

The aftermath of Jonny's downfall, which overshadows Polly's life, drove her to deal with the imperfection of trust and how it can be eroded by the ones we love. When all is over, Polly is a pod of different emotions fighting inside her, introducing her to a labyrinth of self-doubt, guilt and ambiguity.

Just after Jonny' dismissal, Polly's world feels like everything is just spinning out of control. What before seemed solid, the ground beneath her feet now feels dicey, as if she were in a sand dune. She feels as if time has stopped and she has to play the events leading up to Jonny's downfall in her mind. She re-play every little decision, every tiny choice with a mix of regret and relief.

She put her trust in Johnny, had faith in their couple, but now this means a huge hit. She doubts her own ability to have spotted Jonny's trickery and reflexively chastises herself for being gullible. However, the fact that she is just a tool in his hands, which might be never recover from the scars which are so deep.

Nevertheless, in the middle of the chaos, there is a tiny spark of hope; this sign of resilience that never yields to the abyss. Polly finally discovers her inner strength when she realizes that she was the person who contributed even the smallest step in leading Jonny to justice. The idea that the truth will triumph and the imposition of justice, no matter how dark may the situation, is what she is holding on to firmly.

However, the impact of Jonny's downfall is not confined to destruction of the Polly's life only. In the wake of her revelation, the fallout from her example ramble through her community, bears the seed of illusion for others, wipe her homeland clean. Colleagues, friends, acquaintances, everyone face the loss of a friend after the reveal that Jonny was deceitful, trying to work out how they could still represent the person they thought they knew.

The moment of truth is meeting the people, who were her friends, who stood by her despite Jonny's miserable mistakes. She knows the look that is in their eyes, the silence in their voices, and it painfully slices through her. The integrity of the trust she considered unbreakable now becomes brittle, poetically resembling the shattering and collapse of the particles that make it.

By overcoming all of these difficult obstacles, Polly draws closer to the people who care for her and who remain steadfast beside her through this whole traumatic experience. Her family, her friends, and her coworkers come to her rescue whenever she needs them. They always give her what she needs to go forward. Their faith in her provides her with a foundation, connecting her to her supporter during her time of need and letting her know that she does not have to face the situation all by herself.

Between all this mess, Polly discovers snips of order—snips where she sees bits of who she is supposed to become. It comes to her mind that the actual strength is not in stepping away from the trouble, but to learn how to face it, with courage and reshaping. She finds that the trust, though, which has been destroyed can be recovered but requires certain time, bit by brick.

However, Polly is not altogether desolate at the end. She has arrested in the wake of Jonny's misfortune. Her shoulders bear the marks of fighting, the principles that she's learned along the way, and a never-fading certainty that, no matter how deep the darkness may seem to penetrate, the new day will still break to reveal a brighter tomorrow.

As she faces the horizon, Polly is aware of the distance of the journey she will be making and that the road ahead will be winding, full of the unknown and uncharted territory. However, she also understands that she already has that power, that she is resilient, and that she is fearless enough to face any challenge that life presents her. And having that back her up, she took that courageous step forward and smiled trustingly at whatever the future may be.

After the shocking episode between her and her husband, Polly's heart was racing as she found herself standing in the ill-lit room. Oh my god! Her husband, the man she used to love and trust, is there next to the head of police, and he looks right at her with that evil smirk.

As she headed into the room, the bruise still on her but a deeper determination than ever before, she was flooded with conversed feelings of rage, betrayal and the glimmer of hope. This was her time, her chance to meet the person who tried her to put in the darkness.

The chief, a rigid figure with a sincere face, insisted that Polly sit. She did what she was told and her gaze not leaving his face. She could see that his eyes had a tension that clearly showed he was afraid of being found by the farce of bravery.

The big guy made no delay. He was straight away opening a file on his desk and letting it run. It was the time when she sat in her kitchen and listened to her husband talking with the shady guy and the one who paid for her attack. She began to feel a lump in her stomach just as the recording played. This was the evidence she had been looking for all the time that would get her husband punished.

The dismay of her husband's face was in tandem with the screens that were displaying the damning evidence. He attempted to conceal his apprehension, but Polly had a sixth sense for such emotions. This was the precise moment, the final step for her to reveal what had been hidden behind all those years.

However, the chief did something else this time. He played the other tape – her husband's voicemail. The voice came from the recording, closely as that of her husband, asking for a plumber. Polly's heart had a sink feeling as she grasped what the information disclosed.

She was in a state of confusion, and it was hard to form coherent ideas because of it. Why was her husband in one place at one time and in another at the same time? Was he playing a secret game against me?

The chief, who was evidently troubled by her puzzled expression, indicated towards the door. "Oh, silly me!" she exclaimed, as her husband's figure emerged from another door, still injured from their earlier blow-up.

"Hi, sweetie," he remarked, his tone exposed a pretentious attitude.

Polly's mind was buzzing as she was trying to make sense of the hides and goes. Had she been mistaking everything for that particular time? Was she totally right about her husband being innocent?

But then, she realized the horror in husband's eye, the way he was trying to influence her. This wasn't the mannerisms of a harmless man — it was the tricks of a culprit.

And as she realized the truth, tension in Polly seemed to release and she was flooded with relief. She could be gullible, but now she was sure about one fact: her husband was a liar, a man using any means at his disposal to save his own skin.

With reinvigorated will power, Polly addressed herself to the Chief, in a voice that was level and certain. "I want to file charges," she replied. Her eyes were fixed on her husband's face all the time.

The chief nodded his head slowly. He seemed to be deep in thought. "We'll take care of everything," he concluded.

And in this manner Polly suddenly came to the realization of the finality of it all. The fight was not a walk in the park, but the odds had worked in her favor. She had not been a victim anymore — she was a survivor.

Her shoulders got a little lighter as she left the police station that day. She felt

such a relief! She might not comprehend the full extent of the betrayal, that

was not important to her. What is important, was to get on with her life, take

back her life, her independence.

Furthermore, as she took a step out in the bright sunlight, she was convinced

that she was able to handle anything that life would bring. Determined to look

ahead, the head high and the own self-worth recovered, Polly felt ready to take

on a fresh start.

At the conclusion of the passionate two days that have just passed, Polly is

engrossed in a crowd of feelings. She was stunned by the encounter with her

husband, his unfaithfulness, and the fact that the chief of police also figured in

the case. Nevertheless, as I fought through the chaos, there was a gleam of

hope that rose amidst it – a spark of light at the end of a seemingly endless

tunnel.

Despite the torn spirit, Polly still stood with her head up and to boldly face the

truth. She had passed the Hardest trial that one could be put to by the most

Trusted person in her life, but she had also found an inner Force she was never aware existed. This was a courage that grew from trouble, fed by the love that held her together, and driven by the unyielding aid of the people who had stood by her.

Looking at his smoking face, she realized she was as shocked as he was. In a seemingly deadly conclusion, the chief's unveiling that the plumber who passed away in their living room was Jerry was a revelatory twist in this already confusing tale. However, when the hard part came, Polly was unflinching, just as she had always been.

Her eyes met his, and there arose a flash in his pupils—one of recognition—it was the moment when he began to see that the mask he had created fell apart. There were no more Wall of Lies I could lean on anymore, no more Secrets to swept under the rug. In that moment of mental break, Polly found a release, a way to put an end to the struggles she had suffered.

In the sternest way, Polly ended her relationship with her husband. The woman had found him, he stood there before her eyes, all his fantasies gone, fully realized and exposed in his nakedness. We shed off the masks, with no ones to lie to, no fake realities to live in. The silence that followed was deep and vague. It was then that Polly's voice sounded deep and true.

"I'm done," she said, her sentence suggested the finality of the action. "I'm through with the deception, disloyalty, treachery. I'm tired of being forced to believe that all is well when it isn't. I deserve to be treated better and shall not settle for anything less."

When her husband's glance fell to the ground, his mask fell apart under the pressure of her revealed self. He had lost the one thing he thought he could trust—the woman who had been beside him for all the ups and downs of life, and then she proved to be unfaithful to his trust.

The silence affecting the whole room was reflected in the chief's eyes, the living witness to what was coming to pass. With a stony look, his expression was impossible to read and the absence of emotion in his eyes was noticeable Nevertheless, Polly visualized a ray of understanding in his eyes—a feeling of the power and courage she possess to walk out of those lies, which had begun to entangle her since long.

Polly's heart was heavy and she had a new kind of purpose. She turned to leave, tears running down her face. A feeling of weightlessness clutched her inside, a sent of freedom she had never thought she would ever achieve. When she finally walked out into the fresh night breeze, she could feel a kind of release from her soul that was bittersweet—an ending and a new beginning at the same time.

Beyond the window, the world lay outside, infinite in its dimensions, which would become the background for her to project the hues of her recently discovered freedom. Now and then she migrated from those ghosts of her past turning her face to the future which was filled with hope, hope and the hope of new beginnings instead.

In the period after, Polly started her journey of self realisation. A voyage aimed at taking back her identity, her voice and her truth. With the solid backing and encouragement of those nearest and dearest to her, she continued to dust herself off and stayed focused on creating a meaningful and successful life.

Months after the accident, the visible and invisible scars on Polly's body began to heal. She took refuge in the ease and beauty of the ordinary—the sun rays, kisses of loved ones, the sight of a world re-birthed.

But concurrently with all the disorder of her previous life, Polly managed to discover romance—in an entirely different place, with the person she would have never thought about as a match. In the unexpectedly beautiful reflection of warmth and affection, she discovered she was more than just a body, a spirit who saw her scars and yet, loved her for who she was.

Day by day, Polly's heart became lighter while her soul was giving out more and more luminescence. She had sloughed off the demons and shone—a survivor, a warrior, a woman re-born.

And so, in the end, Polly stood there at the door of a new beginning as a living testament to human resilience, courage and of the hope that is firmly planted in our hearts.

The End